## THE SPHINX OF MARS

It rose like a mountain of black stone from the dust. They came upon it in the twilight of the cold martian day—Zarouk and his prisoner, the outworlder who had defied the ancient taboos of the People. The sphinx glittered weirdly in the dying light; even the great *slidar* lizards they rode shied away from the presence of the mountainous sculptured insect. The front of its thorax was a sheer wall of black crystal.

*And in that wall of glistening jet, a doorway yawned!*

# THE CITY
# OUTSIDE THE WORLD

## LIN CARTER

A BERKLEY MEDALLION BOOK
published by
BERKLEY PUBLISHING CORPORATION

*BERKLEY MEDALLION BOOKS are published by*
*Berkley Publishing Corporation*
*200 Madison Avenue*
*New York, N.Y. 10016*

BERKLEY MEDALLION BOOK ® TM 757,375

Printed in the United States of America

Berkley Medallion Edition, OCTOBER, 1977

*For Jack Williamson,*
*the Old Master.*

# Contents

## IV.   OUTSIDE THE WORLD

## V.   AN AGE THAT TIME FORGOT

# I
## Flight from Yeolarn

# 1. The Girl with the Golden Eyes

THEY WERE HUNTING HIM.

You can't stay alive on Mars for very long without developing a sixth sense for such things. And Ryker had stayed alive.

It was nothing obvious or overt the hunters did which caught his attention. They were too wise in the art of manhunting to blunder or expose themselves; no, it was nothing like that.

It was a matter of many small, trifling things. The sound of a footstep in an alley he had believed empty. A shadow against the wall, gone when he glanced at it. A tingle at the back of his neck that told him unseen eyes were watching.

They had been hunting him for a long time, he knew.

And now they were closing in. . . .

Ryker growled a curse under his breath: he had been hunted before, and knew the feeling well. Not that he liked it much.

The worse thing was not that men were after him. That much he could handle, he thought, balling his heavy hands into scarred fists and hunching his broad shoulders so that the great ropes of muscles stood out on his bronzed bare forearms like cables of woven copper wire. No, being hunted did not worry him.

The thing was, *he didn't know why.*

Whenever Ryker came in from the Dustlands to the city, he usually holed up in the native quarter across the old canal. You could live cheap there, if you could stay alive, and one thing was sure: the CA cops couldn't find you, even if they tried.

Cops never go into the Old City of Yeolarn if they can help it. And when they can't help it, well, they don't live long once the narrow walls and shadowy alleyways of the ancient town have closed about them, cutting them off from the bright steel-and-plastic sprawl of the New City across the waterway.

Ryker grinned briefly, baring white teeth in a dark, scarred face. He hated the cops, hated them more than the natives did, he often thought. And that was a lot of hate.

Yeolarn is built like this: on one side of the canal the old-time astronomers back Earthside had named Hydra-otes, the New City rises, all chrome and neon and multi-colored plastic. It is by way of being the capital of Mars; at least that's where the Colonial Administration has its central offices. In the New City live the men and women from Earth—bankers, clerks, accountants, civil and military personnel, doctors, nurses, bureaucrats. In neat rows of prefab, airsealed bungalows, sanitized and sterilized and pressurized, holding the thin, bitter air and the soft, cold dust of old Mars at arm's length.

On the further side of the canal, the Old City rises. It was already old when they laid the cornerstone of Babylon, old when Pharoah's engineers cleared away the sand to start building the Great Pyramid, old before the ice came down over Europe. When Yeolarn was young the British Isles were still attached to the continent, and our ancestors wore furs, wandered the world-wide forests, had yet to domesticate the dog or invent fire.

*Old*—that was Yeolarn. Old beyond our thoughts or dreams. Older by a million years and more than Mohenjo-dara, Ur of the Chaldees, or Jericho. The ages had marched over its squat, nine-sided towers and flattened domes and sleek walls of terracotta-colored native marble, smoothing the sharp edges, wearing the newness away. As house or shrine, temple or palace, slumped into decay under the slow march of the millenia, they were tamped down, and new structures were raised above their dead ruins like tombstones. Yeolarn had been built and rebuilt so many times that it was by now a trackless maze of zigzag alleys, a warren of windowless blind walls, a labyrinth in which a man could hide forever.

When Ryker first stumbled on the fact that he was being watched and followed, he assumed it was the CA cops. It was only a logical assumption, given his record. Gun-running, smuggling, aircar-theft, these were only the more innocuous of the crimes listed in his dossier. So it was natural that his first thought was that the cops were dogging his steps.

That was his first mistake.

So he doubled his tracks, left a few scraps of gear and clothing in the cheap dockside room he had rented, and slunk by furtive, secret ways into the Old City.

That was his second mistake.

Once he had doubled back and forth through the maze of dark, crooked alleys and put himself beyond the ability of the most sharp-nosed of cops to find, he headed across the city towards the old Bazaar of the Lions, bound for the wineshop of Kammu Jha, his favorite joy-house.

That was his third mistake, and it was very nearly fatal.

The public room of the wineshop was long and low ceilinged and roofed with slabs of stone. At one end of the hall gaped the yawning mouth of a huge fireplace, carved out of worn gray stone into the likeness of a dragon's fanged and grinning jaws. Along one wall ran benches.

Small tables stood scattered about in helter-skelter fashion. There was no bar: serving boys fetched orders of wine or ale or the Martian equivalent of brandy from kegs hung on the walls of a back room.

In the stone fireplace, coiled on the flat of the dragon's granite tongue, danced flame. Flame sprung from no ordinary fuel, for coal and wood were rare and precious beyond the dreams of avarice here on this cooling desert world. No, this flame leaped from a flat metal dish like an ewer. Therein lay pooled the ice-green fluid the Martian people call *hiyawa ziu*: "mother of fire." This strange chemical burns like thermite or phosphorus, but slowly, yielding a tremendous store of heat. The People distill it from a porous mineral called *ziuaht*, "firestone."

The room was full of men.

A score or more crouched on the long benches, or sat, hunched with tension, motionless at the tables. They were natives one and all, with the red-copper hide and oblique amber-green eyes of their kind. Under shaven brows, their faces were lean and hard and wolfish. Rings of tooled bronze or beaten copper clasped throat, wrist, biceps. Kiltlike skirts of faded leather shielded belly and thighs; some of these were worked with tartanlike patterns of cross-hatched lines which were the tribal bearings of their nations. Others, however, wore their leather plain, which denoted them as *aoudhha*: "the clanless," men without kin—outlaws, or outcasts, or both.

They paid no attention to Ryker as he came into the wineshop. That was because their attention was rivetted upon the girl who danced before them in an open space. The girl who coiled and glided like the flame that danced upon the stony dragon's tongue that was the hearth.

When Ryker saw her, his attention was seized, too.

She was naked, except for a single strap of gilded

leather that hung down before her loins. Her body was slim and lean and tawny, sinuous as a panther's, and as golden. That rare, pale gold that denotes on Mars the pure breeding of the princely houses of the High Clans.

Her hair was a banner of black silk, floating on the spicy, hot breath of the fire. Her breasts were shallow, rounded, firm, like lustrous, pale fruit. As she danced, moving her loins and torso alone, her feet all but motionless on the pave, her arms were thrust skyward and slightly back, curved at the wrists, held moveless.

She danced—if the writhing undulation could be named with so mundane a verb—with her belly and her breasts and her buttocks.

Ryker sucked in one long breath, and held it until the blood drummed in his temples. His pale and colorless eyes burned coldly from the dark leathern mask of his face. Never had he seen or imagined a dance so rawly savage, yet so exquisitely sensual.

She danced like ripples of moonfire riding the black waters of the old canals; like pattering leaves driven by a moaning and restless wind aprowl through an abandoned courtyard. Her flesh—*crawled*. Her bare breasts panted. Her belly and loins swung in a slow, undulating spiral that was naked invitation.

Her tawny limbs had been rubbed with scented oil until they glowed like amber silks. Then a sparkling dust, like that of crushed mirrors, had been sprinkled across her body. Firelight glittered like powdered gems from every sinuous twist and undulation.

Reluctantly lifting his eyes from the allure of her breasts, Ryker saw that her face was catlike, wide cheeked, elfin, with a small chin and a full-lipped mouth. Her nose was pert, a mere nubbin. Her eyes—

He frowned, then. For she went masked and he could

7

not see her eyes. The visor was of black satin, molded to fit the contours of her face, and it had no eyeholes. Which was strange, he thought, but not very important. With all that sleek, glowing flesh to drink in, he did not have to see her eyes.

And that was his last mistake.

She danced to the pittering of drums and the wail of a small pipe. An old, bony man clenched the drums between gaunt knees, where he squatted to one side of the dragon's-mouth fireplace. His gnarled, knobbed hands made dry, erratic music.

The pipe was held by a naked boy of perhaps twelve, who leaned with gamine grace against a pillar. The thin, wailing cry of his pipe was like a lost soul in torment, sobbing from the throat of hell. The shrill, raw pain of the sound, and the sadness in it, raised the nape hairs on Ryker's neck and made the skin on his bare arms creep.

And then, suddenly—quite suddenly—the dance was done.

The girl froze in her last position, then turned and glided away, shrugging through bead curtains that tinkled across a narrow stone doorway. The old man ceased his pattering and climbed stiffly to his feet and hobbled out after the girl. The naked boy took the pipe away from his mouth, grinned impishly, and picked up a copper bowl from a low table and went around the room from man to man.

The men stood or sat, breathing heavily, still staring with hot eyes at the empty space where the girl had writhed. They barely noticed the boy, merely plucking a coin from their belt pouch as he paused in front of each, clinking his bowl remindingly.

When the boy stopped in front of Ryker, the Earthman looked him over slowly, with bemused eyes, coming out of his trance painfully. As he dropped a coin in the bowl his eyes caught sight of something on the boy's naked chest. Just above the heart and just below the nipple an emblem had once been tattooed. Efforts had been made to erase that which had been needled there, but the smooth, sleek flesh caught the gleam of the firelight in such a way that Ryker could see marks of the needles, even though the pigment had been erased.

It was an odd sign, vaguely familiar: a crouching, many-legged creature, vaguely like an insect. And winged, the many wings folded against its slope of thorax and pod. Weird and strange, and curious.

Mischief gleamed in the boy's eyes, and a trace of contempt, as he looked at the Earthman and knew him for what he was, a hated *F'yagha*, an Outworlder. But he did not reject the coin. Turning on his heels, his round little bottom cocked impudently, he swaggered from the room. Shouldering through the tinkling bead curtains, he vanished after the old man and the naked dancer, and was gone.

Now the serving boys came out from wherever they had been hiding, with ceramic pitchers full of wine. Gradually, the numb trance faded and men began to shuffle, grunt, move again.

Ryker accepted a bowl of sharp red wine and drank it thirstily.

His mind was busy with something that bothered him.

It was the girl, or, rather, her *eyes*.

As she had glided past him through the bead curtains, one strand had caught upon the corner of her visor and stripped it from her face. And he had gotten one swift, transient glimpse of her eyes.

They were huge and thick lashed, those eyes, tip-tilted and inexpressibly lovely.

9

And they were *golden*. Golden as puddles of hot metal poured by the jeweler for the making of a precious brooch.

And that was strange. For the People (as the Martian natives call their race) have, most commonly, eyes of amber, sometimes of liquid brown, and even occasionally of emerald. But never of gold. Or never that Ryker knew or had ever seen.

She could not have been an Earthsider, not with that tawny skin and blacksilk hair and snub-nosed cat's face. Nor a Martian, not with those eyes of molten gold.

Which meant she was of an unknown race. . . .

Or from an unknown world!

## 2. Whispering Shadows

HE HAD BEEN on Mars a dozen years, had Ryker, but he was no Colonist.

In the early days, Earthside governments had found few of their people willing to emigrate to the distant, dry, hostile planet. So they had forced emigration by making it a legal punishment for certain crimes. In the same manner, and for much the same reason, Britain had once dumped its unwanted and condemned on the shores of Australia, dooming these unfortunates to a lifetime of penal servitude in a prison the size of a continent, whose walls were oceans, with storms for guards.

What Ryker had done back on Earth to merit deportation does not concern us here. But he had not been a criminal, exactly, unless adherence to unpopular political philosophies be deemed a crime. Once he had been, in his way, something of a patriot. Once he had placed the common good above his own comfort and security. But no longer.

Here, on this ancient desert world, merely to survive is difficult enough. To *live* is something else again. And Ryker had lived, which is to say, he had been made to do things he would not have chosen to do, had conditions been otherwise.

But here, at least, he was free. If Mars, in the beginning, had been a prison, it was a prison without walls, where the condemned could freely come and go as they willed. The only thing they could not do was return to

11

Earth again. Only the most serious crimes merited real imprisonment. Those who, back on Earth, had been judged homicidal murderers, political assassins, terrorists, or dedicated revolutionaries, were sent here to sweat and scrabble in the barium mines until death released them from their chains.

Men such as Ryker were not thought dangerous enough to be locked away in that living hell. There was no need for Earthmen to toil like animals in the black, bottomless mines. For that, the Colonial Administration had the natives. True, they were human enough, the People—although, perhaps, their remotest racial ancestor, in the dim beginnings of time, had been feline whereas ours was simian. Once they had been a mighty race, the builders of a high civilization, the proud inheritors of a noble tradition of art, literature and philosophy. But that great heritage had dwindled and perished during the early Pleistocene.

Mars was old—*old.* As her green oceans dried and shrank, as her rich atmosphere thinned, as her internal fires cooled, that which had been lush meadow and forestland once, became dry, powdery desert. No longer could the red world support her teeming life, so that life . . . died.

What was left was in time reduced to savagery, to barbarism. The few remnants of her proud empires inexorably dwindled to ragged, starveling outlaw bands, who huddled for warmth in the ruined shells of what once had been brilliant and populous cities, and thus Mars broke and humbled the last of her children. The People had lost the dice-roll of destiny; and Earthlings had never liked losers. So, while a few scientists studied their dying traditions and strove to rescue from oblivion their half-forgotten sciences, the more brutal—or more practical—of the uninvited visitors from the green world nearer to the

12

sun regarded them as ignorant savages to be ruthlessly exterminated, cruelly exploited, casually enslaved.

It was an old, old story back on Earth. But history tends to repeat itself, and while glittering socialites in sophisticated capitals glibly murmur of basic rights and freedoms, things are done on far frontiers that would shock them into unbelieving, bewildered horror.

Frontier garrisons are frontier garrisons. Life is hard and survival is chancy. And dead natives tell no tales.

Thus the People, by now, had good reason to hate and distrust the Outworlder colonists and to avoid commerce with them. Luckily, Mars is wide and most of it is uninhabited and hostile wilderness. So, while the Colonists clung together, holding the thin cold air and the dry sterile deserts at bay behind their plastic inflatable domes and pressure pumps, the Martian natives had all their world to roam free, and only a few of the hardiest among the Colonials risked leaving the snug security of their plastic warrens for the hazards which await the unwary beyond the half-dozen colonies.

Ryker knew there was no going back, and had determined to survive in any way he could. The air of Mars is thin and starved for oxygen as it is for moisture, but there was a way Earthsider lungs and blood chemistry could be subtly modified to endure it without cumbersome thermal suits and respirators. This method, the Mishubi-Yakamoto regimen, cost money. But with it, Ryker would be free to wander the surface of Mars for as long as he could stay alive.

So he got the money. Never mind how. If, in getting it, he bent a few laws to the breaking point, and filled a fat dossier in the Criminal Files of the Colonial Administration, the getting made him freer than before. The paradox is but one of those Mars affords its visitors.

The People themselves are by way of being rebels against CA law, which makes them outcasts and criminals, fair game for any cop with a grudge. The only *F'yagha* they permit a wary sort of welcome into their towns or encampments are, similarly, criminals and outcasts. Ryker had, early on, won the friendship of the native clans, or as much friendship as any Earthsider can win, which isn't much. Call it toleration if you will, and not friendship. At least he was free to come and go among the People with no questions asked, so long as he kept to himself, left their women alone, kept away from their holy places, and did not meddle in their affairs.

What he did upon leaving the joy-house was dangerous, very dangerous. For he was breaking those unwritten laws he had so scrupulously observed all these years.

And the penalty was death.

Keeping well to the shadows, he was following the dancing girl, the old man and the boy.

Why he was doing this he could not have explained even to himself. Call it curiosity, if you like, or a hunch. But outcasts like Ryker do not live very long on Mars unless they develop that sixth or seventh sense that permits them to smell out danger before it strikes, and profit before the money is laid out on the table.

It was that glimpse of the girl's golden eyes, coupled with that half-erased tattoo on the boy's smooth breast that made Ryker's extra sense tingle. For he knew enough of Martian traditions and history to know that in the old time, when the great Martian civilization still basked in its golden twilight and ages before the High Clans and princely bloodlines had mixed and become mongrelized, the lords and nobles of the pure blood had looked forth from golden eyes such as those which transformed the girl's heart-shaped face into a marvel.

And he had seen that insect sign before.

Once, years before, in the Eastern Dustlands, he had found and rifled an age-old tomb. Time had buried it deep beneath bone-dry, talcum-fine sand; a chance windstorm —rare on the desert world, though not entirely unheard of—had laid bare the black marble door to the hillside tomb.

Within had been few pieces of gold and fewer gems, but many artifacts of interest to the scientists. And in those days, before the police dossier which carried Ryker's name had become quite so fat, he could still come and go in Syrtis Port or Sun Lake City without suspicion or harrassment. So he had sold the tomb artifacts one by one to the historians and the professors interested enough in XT archaeology to ignore the fact that they were purchasing stolen goods. One by one he had sold the little ceramic jars and figurines and symbolic tools and weapons. All but one piece were gone. That one he had kept for himself, for some reason he could not quite put a name to.

Perhaps it was just a whim. Or perhaps he took a fancy to the thing he had found clasped tight to the bony breast of the Martian mummy, folded tight in withered arms. Or maybe he thought of it as a souvenir, or a good-luck piece. Whatever the reason, it had slept above his heart, suspended on a thong around his neck, all these years, in a little leathern bag.

It was a seal of slick, glassy black stone, sleek and glistening as obsidian, but heavier than marble. It was a small thing—the palm of one hand could cover it. Small or not, it was a mystery. For no jeweler or geologist to whom he had given shavings from it could name the dense, ebon

15

crystal from which it was made. And none of the experts to whom he lent a rubbing copy could read the characters in the unknown and unclassified language which ran around the edge of one side of the seal.

On the reverse of that seal, deeply embossed in high relief, was a figure, a figure like a fantastic, crouching insect—but such an insect as our fields and forests had never housed. Such an insect as Mars itself was never home to, even in its greener ages.

But by the shreds and scraps salvaged from the old traditions and sagas and mythologies he knew that strange, crouching insect. In the nearly forgotten lore of the People the creature was known as *The Pteraton.* The name means "The Guardian of the Gateway"; but it should have been named The Enigma.

Two thousand miles from the dark, narrow alleys of Yeolarn, its huge stony likeness crouched amid the waste, like some gigantic and mythological Sphinx. A full hundred yards it measured from beaked, antenna-crowned face to tapering, cylindrical thorax-tip. And no man—Martian or Earthsider scientist alike—could say who built it, or when, or why. Or what it signified.

*The Sphinx of Mars* the Earthside newscasters called it. And like that other vast Enigma that has crouched for ages in the deserts beyond Gizeh, while empires waxed and waned, its mystery has never been solved.

Now why, wondered Ryker to himself, was the likeness of the Stone Enigma he had found graven on a black seal from an ancient tomb, why had it once been tattooed upon the naked breast of a nameless, homeless, clanless gutter-snipe of a native Martian boy?

The shadows grew thicker in the maze of alleys that was the Old City.

As the three glided purposefully on before him, Ryker noticed with distress that they were no longer alone in these narrow ways, save for the shadows.

For he heard the faint shuffle of sandal leather in the black, yawning mouths of alleys as they went past them—the scrape of boot soles, the faint tread of furtive footsteps.

Glancing back over his shoulder, he saw a movement among the shadows, as of men gathering for some unknown purpose.

They were silent and grimly purposeful. They kept a good distance between themselves and the three they followed, but they kept up with them. They neither let them get too far ahead, nor too far behind.

And now the dancing girl, the old man and the naked boy could be seen to hesitate at the entrance to alleys, to turn aside, to falter. And it slowly dawned upon Ryker that the three he followed were being . . . *herded*.

He looked back over his shoulder at their pursuers. There were very many of them and they were curiously unspeaking.

They looked to him like a mob. And mobs are as unpredictable, as potentially dangerous, as unruly and as given to sudden whims of violence on Mars as back on Earth.

Despite the cold, dry air of the evening, sweat broke out upon Ryker's brow and the skin crawled horribly on the nape of his neck.

He began to wish, and that most fervently, that he had never let that idle curiosity, that vagrant impulse, lead him out of the tavern to follow the girl with the golden eyes and the boy whose breast bore the Mark of Mystery into the furtive, meandering, shadow-steeped back alleys of old Yeolarn.

But he had, and there was no turning back now. He

sensed the mood of the mob behind him. They were after the girl and her companions, not after him. But they would not permit him to escape, either. Whatever lay ahead—towards whatever trap or cul-de-sac they were herding the three fugitives—no witness would be permitted to get away unmolested.

Especially, no *F'yagha* witness.

Ryker growled a bitter curse deep in his throat, and his fingers curled about his gun butt. His hard face grew bleak. His lips thinned, and his cold, pale eyes went hunting restlessly from side to side, for a doorway, an open arcade, a flight of worn steps. But no avenue of escape was left open, he knew within his heart. Silent men stood deep in the shadows, blocking every way out of the maze.

They came at last into an open square which was walled on three sides by sheer stone surfaces, unbroken by gate or archway.

At the entrance to this cul-de-sac, Ryker halted and stood aside against the nearer wall in the black shadow of an overhanging second-story balcony, hoping not to be seen.

The girl, the old man, and the boy, stopped, too, realizing they were trapped and could go no further.

The silent mob halted at the entrance to the little courtyard, and stood motionless, blacker shadows amid the darkness of the alley. Ryker drew his gun and hid it in a fold of his cloak and stood there sweating, wishing himself a thousand miles away. He smelled an execution in the air, and the stench of it was fearsome and ugly.

And then the shadows, which stood ranked motionless, began to . . . *whisper.* Ryker cocked his ears to catch the unfamiliar word. It was rarely heard, even in the vilest dens of Mars, but it was not unknown to him.

18

*"Zhaggua!"* the shadows were whispering.

The word was blunt and unlovely, and they spat it like a curse.

*"Zhaggua! Zhaggua!—Zhaggua!"*

The girl stood, naked under her fringed long-shawl, facing the faceless shadow-throng proudly, masked face lifted fearlessly, and took the ugly word full in the face like a glob of spittle. She took it unflinchingly, Ryker noticed. And even here, with death inches away and only moments in the future, he felt the pure, sweet, singing spirit of her, and he marveled at it. The manhood within him responded to the unconscious grace of her slim, poised body, her thrusting breasts outlined under the thin silken stuff of the shawl, and the pride and scorn eloquent in the fearless lift of that masked face.

*"Zhaggua!"*

The shadows were inching closer now, the glitter of catlike eyes intent on their prey. And the whispering rose to a chant as the ugly strange name, the ugly word, was spat forth. The smell of the mob was rank and vile in Ryker's nostrils, and the name of that smell was *hate*. But the reek of fear was in that sharp stench, too. And that was strange.

For why should the mob, many men strong, fear a slim girl, an old man, and a child?

But yet another question seethed through the turmoil of Ryker's thoughts. And it was the strangest mystery of all.

For the vile, guttural word—*Zhaggua*—had a meaning. A meaning lost in the dim vistas of the past, shrouded behind old mysteries and forgotten legends, veiled in the obscurity of remote and unremembered aeons.

It was a dirty word, that ugly grunt of sound. It was a curse, an obscenity, like "nigger" or "wop" or "Commie."

It was a word which had once been applied to a people lost in time's far, forgotten dawn.

It was a name that had not been used against a living man in millions of years.

It meant . . . *Devil*!

"*Zhaggua—Zhaggua—Zhaggua!*" the mob chanted, and now Ryker saw they held stones and bricks cupped in eager, trembling hands. Stones, heavy stones, to beat down that slim, proud, fearless, warm gold body. To beat and break and pulp that sleek, perfumed flesh.

But *why*?

*Devil—Devil—Devil!* The mob growled as it surged forward, stones lifted, to kill.

# 3. Red Thirst

RYKER CURSED, SHRUGGED his cloak back over his shoulders, and stepped forward. Knowing himself for a fool, he lifted his heavy guns. There was nothing else that he could do, after all. He had been many things in his time, and had done those things that tarnish the soul and harden the heart. He had lied, cheated, thieved, and he had killed for hire. But one thing he had never done, and could never do, and live at peace with himself thereafter.

He had never stood idly by and watched a woman be torn apart by a mob.

The shrill yammer of his power guns shrieked as they cut through the growling of the mob.

The thick shadows were split asunder, quite suddenly, by a cold, unearthly light. It was blue-white, that glare of fierce electric fire. And men fell before the blaze of those twin guns as wheat stalks fall before the keen-bladed scythe.

The mob was as brave as mobs usually are. That is to say, each man lost his own fear in the lust for violence which gripped them all, even as each felt his individuality submerged in the oneness that was the mob.

Therefore, each man was only as brave as those around him.

The mob was one animal by now, one huge animal with many parts and one desire in its hot heart—the red thirst for blood. But before the yammering shriek of those guns the mob dissolved into its component units. Those units were only men—alone, individual now, isolated from the mob mentality, and terribly vulnerable to the cold fire that spat from the grim muzzles of Ryker's guns. The men had only bricks and stones and broken bottles in their hands, for power guns were forbidden to the People and were hard to come by in the Old City.

And bricks and stones and bottles weighed little in the balance against the sizzling death vomited forth by the twin guns held rock-steady in Ryker's hard, scarred fists.

A dozen men, maybe more, lay dead on the dusty cobblestones that paved the plaza. And the evil smell of burnt flesh was thick in the nostrils of those who lived.

The red thirst faded in their hearts, and in its place came fear. They licked their lips. They hesitated. They gave little, quick sideways glances at each other. And they hesitated. Had the mob been goaded on by a leader, it might still have been rallied. But there was no leader to stand forth and confront the bright death held now in check by a finger's pressure.

The mob began to crumble, peeling away in scuttling, shadowy figures. First, the rear ranks melted away as if by sorcery. Then from the sides, and men turned away and slunk off into the black ways of the little, crooked alley.

Finally there were none in all the little plaza, save for Ryker, the girl, her two companions, and the dead.

Ryker drew a long, ragged breath, and put his guns back in their worn leather holsters, and his heart began to beat again.

He turned to face the girl, who still stood proudly before her companions, and who had not moved or spoken.

He cleared his throat and spoke. Some whim made him speak not in the harsh sibilants of the gutter lingo he would have used, but in that old and finer variant of the Tongue spoken only by the warrior princelings of the High Blood.

For something told him these were no folk of the Low Clans.

He said, "They will not have gone far. I think they will be waiting for us back at the place where many black alleys open on the way we came. So we must be gone from here, and quickly, and that by another way."

For the first time the masked girl spoke, and her voice was like the music made by the chiming of many little silver bells. Clear and sweet was the music of that voice, but cold as metal.

"And how would you have us go from here, Outworlder? Through the very walls themselves? For there are neither doors nor windows."

Ryker indicated the balcony at the far end of the plaza, in whose shadow he had stood when the mob first charged. The girl nodded without words. He made as if to help her ascend the wall, but she ignored the hand he proffered. With the kick of her long dancer's legs she sprang into the air, caught ahold of the bottom ledge, and swung herself nimbly up and upon the carven stone balustrade.

Ryker lifted the old man up to her and between them they got him over the rail. He was very light, his arms and legs as thin as sticks. He said nothing.

The naked boy gave Ryker one bright glance of pure mockery and mischief, then sprang as lightly as an acrobat upon the Earthling's shoulders and gained the balcony. Ryker jumped up and caught the carved rail and heaved himself up and over it. Despite the lower gravity of Mars, the exertion left him red faced and puffing. He was unaccustomed to such acrobatics. The boy giggled, but the old man and the girl said nothing.

The small, roofed balcony gave way to a second-floor room, but the way was barred by shutters, tightly closed and locked from within. On Earth the shutters would have been of wood, but here on the desert world where wood was almost as rare as water, they were of thin, fretted and carven stone which resembled lucent alabaster. The stone was thin and fragile. Ryker kicked the shutters in with one thrust of his booted feet.

They crawled through the opening he had made, and found themselves in a long-unused room, thick with soft dust, the air of which was sour from old cooking smells. A few pieces of ancient furniture stood along the walls, covered with cloths. A tall door of worn metal, also locked, gave way to a narrow landing and a flight of steps leading down to the street level.

There were no windows which gave forth upon the next street, but eye-chinks were cut into the stone walls to either side of the main door in the Martian manner. The view through these peepholes suggested that the street beyond was empty of men. But Ryker had learned caution in a hard school, and felt uncertain that the way to freedom was quite as clear as it seemed to be.

"Do you and your friends have a place of refuge where you will be safe?" he asked. The girl shrugged slim shoulders under her silken shawl.

"A purchased room in the House of the Three Djinns, near the Caravan Gate," she murmured listlessly. Ryker thought quickly. He knew the place she meant, an old hostelry whose courtyard was guarded by three stone colossi called Ushongti—djinnlike giants out of Martian legend. The Caravan Gate was to the north of the Old City. The twistings and turnings of the winding alleys had confused him, and he could not say for certain how much of the city they must traverse to reach the caravanserai.

"But it will be no longer safe for us," the girl added in her sing-song voice, cool and sad as faint chimes heard at twilight.

24

"Why so?"

She shrugged again.

"Now that the *hualatha* have found us," she murmured, "there is no safe refuge for such as we in all of Yeolarn."

By *hualatha,* she meant "holy ones," or priests. A cold wind was blowing up Ryker's spine, and, again, he wished he had never obeyed that whim of curiosity that had led him to follow the girl and her companions out into the night.

"Was it the *hualatha* who set the mob on you?" he asked.

"Of course," she said. "Did you not notice the *hua* among the fallen?"

Ryker thought back to the litter of the dead they had left in the little square behind this house. He had noticed that one of the men he had gunned down wore black, cowled robes. Now that he thought about it, the corpse had been of a man with a shaven pate, like a priest. He almost remembered the silver sigils clipped to the man's earlobes in the priestly manner.

*It was bad, and it's getting even worse,* he thought to himself bitterly. Bad enough to be caught following a native woman through the streets at night—for that, the People had been known merely to castrate *F'yagha.* And to come between a native mob and its prey—to beam a dozen down—that was death. And not a swift or easy death, either. But to kill a priest . . .

Ryker shuddered. The penalty for that he did not even know. Nor did he want to.

But he had gained a piece of information. It was the priests who had driven the mob against these three. They must be heretics of some kind, defilers of shrines, perhaps tomb robbers. And if the *hualatha* knew where they were,

25

the girl was right. There was no hiding place anywhere in the Old City that was safe for them. And no place for Ryker to hide either. For there could not be so many Outworlders in Yeolarn that Ryker's identity would not swiftly be learned by those who had hunted the girl.

The only safety lay in flight. But flight to where? And how?

The New City across the canal might afford a safe enough haven for the dancing girl and her party, but not for Ryker. They had hounded him out of the New City, and by this time the way back was surely closed to him. His only chance of seeing the sun rise tomorrow lay in getting out of Yeolarn entirely. And, perhaps, their only chance as well. For native priests can come and go in the New City pretty much as they please.

Ryker began to sweat again. He could feel the perspiration trickle down his ribs under his thermals. He leaned against the stone wall and tried desperately to think. The smooth stone was cold and slick against his brow.

"Do you have any idea just where we are now?" he asked.

The girl put her hand to her mouth tentatively. She tilted her head on one side as if listening to some faint sound to which his ears were deaf.

"Near the Processional Way, I think," she said thoughtfully. "It should be through the next alley. We are a square or two from the Bazaar—the Lesser, not the Great. That means the quickest way out of the city would be the Gate of the Dragons—"

Ryker felt his heart quicken. The Gate of the Dragons! Very near that gate was the house of Yammak, a dealer in riding beasts he knew from the old days. And Yammak owed him a favor or two. If they could reach the house of

26

Yammak without being discovered, and if Yammak was there, and could procure *slidars* for the four of them, and provisions, too, then there was a chance they might get out of Yeolarn alive.

It wasn't much of a chance, Ryker knew. A slim chance, at best. But slim or not, it was a whole lot better than no chance at all!

The boy had been shifting his weight from one foot to the other, restlessly. Now he tugged on the hem of the girl's scarf for her attention. She turned her masked head towards him.

"Men are coming, Valarda!" the boy chirped. "Many men. Down the street, there—"

*Valarda . . . so that was her name? It suited her well, that name. In the High Tongue it meant "Golden Bells."* . . .

Ryker shook his head as if to clear his mind of distracting thoughts. It was time to think swiftly, and to act even more swiftly.

"They will have crept back to see if we are still in the square," he said. "Probably by going over the rooftops. At any rate, they will have seen the broken screen by now. They will know that we got away through the balcony. They may even be in the house by this time. We must—"

"The cellar!" the girl said, sharply, in the manner of one who has just remembered something.

"Eh?"

"The crypts," she said impatiently. "There will be a grating beneath the house leading into the old sewer tunnels! The houses in this quarter are old enough to have been built over the sewers which once drained into the ancient seas. We can follow the tunnels beneath the bazaar, and reach the Gate of the Dragons that way!"

"But how will we know which way to—" Ryker started to ask bewilderedly, then closed his lips to the unspoken question. He had forgotten that he was in the company, not of men like himself, but of three of the People. And the People have from of old an uncanny sense of direction that never falters or betrays them.

The girl now took the lead in some unspoken way that even Ryker did not pause to question. She whipped off her black silk mask impatiently, as if it were no longer needed. Then, followed by the boy and the old man, with Ryker blundering along in the rear, she searched until she found a low door which led down beneath the street level into the crypts and vaults which were commonly built under native houses as ancient as this one.

Ryker followed, but without enthusiasm. They told unpleasant tales of the old crypts beneath the houses in this ancient quarter, and of unwholesome things that squirmed and slithered through the black, foul darkness of the tunnels below this part of the city. They were unhealthy, those black tunnels that had been burrowed underneath the cities of Mars before his Earthling ancestors had entered into the Stone Age.

But he had little choice but to follow after Valarda and her companions, if he wanted to live out this night.

For the priests had aroused the mob again, it seemed, and had fanned back into fierce existence that hot red thirst to kill. As he went stumbling down the worn stone steps that led down and down into the black depths beneath the house, he could hear them howling down the hollow canyon of the street, and the thud of the first blows against the tall and narrow door of ancient metal echoed and reechoed after them.

He had stifled the mob's thirst for murder once that night, with the bright fury of his guns. But the trick would not work a second time, he knew. For now the faceless shadows that howled down the night-dark streets and hunted them would be armed with swords and knives, and with those tubelike dart guns with which the People were such deadly and unerring marksmen.

## 4. Beyond the Dragon Gate

OF THEIR NIGHTMARISH journey through the foul and low-roofed tunnels, Ryker could remember but little in the aftertimes. The stone floor underfoot was slick, worn smooth by the passage of waters which had rushed down the black throat of these sewers on their way to join oceans that were legends a million years before Egypt.

No waters rushed here now, but there was moisture, of a sort, enough to sustain mould and lichen and sprouting, tubular fungus. These flaccid growths squelched unpleasantly underfoot, and his boots crushed them to a vile stinking slime as he blundered down the black passages, half-bent to avoid scraping his head against the low curve of the roof.

It had not been hard to locate the entrance to the labyrinth of underground tunnels. The door to the crypts they barred with a massive length of heavy iron which leaned against a wall at the head of the stairway, conveniently at hand for that very purpose, perhaps.

The boy had found the barred grating in a corner of the crypts. It had rusted into place over the ages, and it required a bolt from Ryker's guns—the focus narrowed to needle-beam width—to loosen it. The boy's name was Kiki, it seemed. The old man's name was Melandron or so the girl called him.

Once they had lowered themselves down through the floor grating and dropped to the floor of the tunnelways below, they found themselves in an unlighted gloom so completely impenetrable that, to Ryker, it was like being struck totally blind.

Luckily, the natives of Mars, who trace the descent of their race from a quadrupedal feline shaped by the Gods into manlike form and by Them ensouled, inherit from this legendary First Ancestor the very catlike ability to see in the dark. Ryker could not have traversed the black labyrinth with any speed at all, alone. The boy, Kiki, shrilling an impolite word of abuse, impatiently came scrambling back for the Earthling, seized him by the hand, and led him into the black gloom at a breakneck pace.

The hand was small and strong and calloused and very dirty. But without it, Ryker could not have moved a foot through the darkness without feeling every inch of the way.

He was very grateful they were taking him with them, instead of abandoning him and leaving him behind to his own fate.

It did not occur to Ryker, until very long after, to wonder why they bothered to bring him along at all. . . .

After what seemed to Ryker like interminable hours of crawling through the pitch-black tunnels, but which was more likely well under an hour's time, the girl imperiously called a halt.

At intervals, the low tunnel roof was broken by a circular opening which gave upon a vertical shaft. These shafts were like the one through which they had entered the underground tunnel system in the first place. They gave forth upon the cryptlike spaces beneath the houses, and sometimes they led to the surface of the street itself, where thin plates of metal covered them, like manhole covers in the streets of Earth.

To ascend the vertical shaft was harder than going down

into one, as Ryker found when Valarda halted their progress. You had to brace your feet against one side of the shaft and press your back and shoulders against the opposite side, then inch your way up. There was no other way to do it, because there were neither handholds nor footholds.

Ryker inched his way up the shaft first, and broke the seal which held the plate in place with one heave of his burly shoulders. Climbing out, he discovered himself to be just within the black mouth of a narrow and high-walled alley, very near the house of Yammak. He stretched out flat on his belly and reached down with one arm to clasp the boy's hand. Kiki came scrambling up like a monkey to squat on his little bottom, watching Ryker with bright, amused, malicious eyes as he helped the old man, Melandron, to the street.

As for Valarda, she again ignored the assistance of his hand, and climbed the shaft swiftly and easily, her fingers and bare, wriggling toes finding holds he could have sworn were not there.

They made their way to the house of Yammak without encountering anyone. The night was dark and clear, the stars blazing like an emperor's ransom in diamonds flung out upon black velvet. The twin moons of Mars were both aloft by this hour, which was near to dawn, but were virtually invisible in the sky. Even under the best of conditions, it was difficult to find the two moons with the unaided eye, due to their small size and low albedo.

Yammak was at home, and in his present mood Ryker found it easy to gain his cooperation. Whether it was his memory of old favors still unrepaid, or the cold glint in Ryker's eyes and the way his hard fingers brushed his gun butts, Yammak proved eager to help them on their way. While his woman gathered food and drink and found sleeping furs and other necessities for them, Yammak escorted Ryker and Valarda to the *slidar* pens in the back, where they selected steeds. It was decided that Ryker and Valarda would ride separately mounted, while old Melandron and the boy shared a third beast, with a fourth to serve as pack animal.

Well before moonset the four brutes were saddled and provisioned, and the little party slunk out through the open and unguarded gate between the two stone dragons which so markedly resembled the great saurians that had prowled the murky, steaming fens of Earth's forgotten Mesozoic.

A purse of gold had changed hands, but Ryker depended on more than gold to seal the lips of Yammak. For the fat, beardless, voluble little man had recognized the three who accompanied the Earthling. He had sucked in his breath between discolored teeth at his first good look at them, and his eyes had gone round and frightened.

Oh, he would keep his mouth shut, would Yammak the *slidar* trader! For if he dared so much as to hint that it had been he who had helped the three *zhaggua* to elude their hunters and to escape into the Dustlands, those who hunted them would close the mouth of Yammak forever.


Among the many things he hated about Mars, Ryker most of all hated *slidars.*

The rangy, splay-footed, ungainly beasts were four footed, but there all resemblance to horses ended. They were reptilian, of course—Mars has hardly any mammals and no birds or insects, other than lice—and the crimson, snake-tailed creatures move with a shambling, splay-footed, loose-jointed stride that is peculiarly uncomfortable.

It is not for nothing that the gaunt, big-shouldered, ill-tempered brutes are named *slidars.* The word means "lopers" in the Tongue; and lope they do, with an ambling, jolting rhythm more like that of a fat, stumbling hound dog than anything else on four feet.

Ryker, however, gritted his teeth and clung to the saddle horn and gave the brute its head, allowing it to make all possible speed. He did not begin to breathe easily, or rein the beast in to a more comfortable trot until the last lights of Yeolarn had died behind them in the dark.

Then, and only then, did he slow their advance and begin to consider where they might go.

Yeolarn is the northernmost of the Earth colonies, and sits smack on the 250th Meridian in the center of the Thoana Palus. It is at least eleven hundred miles from Syrtis Port, which is the nearest colony to it, and to the north illimitable empty wastes of Dustland and dead rocky plateaux stretch to the Pole itself.

When they rode out of the Dragon Gate, they had headed due north, Ryker knew. They were now in one of the talcum-soft desert regions called "Dustlands," an empty space on the map which the old Earth astronomers had filled in with the name Aetheria. Due east was an even broader expanse of powdery desert called Cebrenia, which stretched on for twelve hundred miles or so before the mesalike bulk of Propontis rose to block the way.

West, however, they would only have to ride three hundred miles or less to reach the low, rocky hills of Alcyonius Nodus. There, at least, they could find shelter in the caves which the tides of ancient oceans had cut into the cliffs which had once been the coastline of an old continent. And, perhaps, they could find food as well.

He turned to his companions to suggest this, but decided to delay the question until morning, now not long away. For the night had been long and busy. None of them

34

had enjoyed any sleep, and precious little rest, and they were all wearied from their exertions. Indeed, the old man swayed weakly in the saddle, and the girl sat her mount with head low, shoulders bent, slumped dispiritedly.

"Let's dismount here, have something to eat, and snatch a few hours sleep," he suggested.

The girl looked up quickly, her golden eyes filled with fear.

"Is it safe? Perhaps we are pursued—"

Ryker shook his head.

"They'll have found where we entered the sewers, having broken down the cellar door by now, surely," he grunted. "But there's no way they can tell which way we went, or where we came up to the street. Those sewers run for miles and miles, and I replaced the plate that sealed the street exit. And Yammak will not talk."

"How can you be sure of that?"

He grinned, wolfishly, and explained. The girl nodded wearily, satisfied, and got down from her *slidar*.

Wrapped in the warm cloaks supplied by Yammak's woman, they hungrily devoured cold sliced meat, dry bread and preserved jellies, washed down by a frugal swallow of red wine.

They slept that night like the dead, huddled together for warmth.


The air of Mars is thin, and cold, and dry. So dry that it sucks the moisture from your tissues, and so cold that it makes the air atop Everest humid by comparison. And so thin, so oxygen starved, that it is hardly enough to sustain life.

Indeed, when the first Earthsider colonists and explorers came they muffled themselves within airsuits and wore

35

pressure masks, and domed their towns with plastic bubbles. But soon the men of science set to work upon the problem. Earthsiders would never have more than a toehold on this world if they must wear suits and masks in order to live. Since Mars was too vast by far to be terraformed, men themselves were forced to become acclimated.

The first clue came from the Martians themselves. They were warm-blooded hominids of obvious mammalian descent—human to a dozen decimal places—and, somehow or other, they managed to survive.

Biochemists, studying the natives, found out how nature had adapted them to survival under these conditions, and, in time, learned how to modify the body chemistry of the colonists to conform to this harsh environment. The series of operations was expensive, and permanent, but Ryker was damn glad he had bought them. Otherwise, he could not have lasted long in the Dustlands, away from the domed cities of his kind.

But even with his body chemistry adapted to Mars, some precautions were necessary. The thermals he wore were of tough, wear-resistant synthetic, and helped retain his body heat. The pressure still he should have brought with him, and would have, had he known in advance he was in for some overland travel, would have squeezed enough moisture from the rubbery plants that carpeted the so-called "canals" to sustain him without dangerous dehydration.

Lacking it, he was in trouble.

This did not become evident until morning, when he woke to find his throat and the inside of his mouth as dry as blotting paper, and an ache in his sinuses that presaged difficulties to come. A swig or two from his canteen helped, but the water it held would not last for long.

They mounted and rode out.

Valarda and her companions, being natives, did not feel the lack of water as badly as Ryker did. Over the millions of years since Mars first lost her oceans and began to dry up, evolution had adapted the Martians to a lesser need for moisture and an ability to retain moisture superior to that of Earthsider bodies. For instance, Martians do not perspire. Also, their glands produce epidermal oils which tend to seal body moisture within, preventing its evaporation.

Still, in time they would all need fresh water, or they would begin to die that most horrible of all deaths—death through dehydration.

All that day they rode on, heading almost due northwest, for in the Dustlands it is usually possible to travel in straight lines—"as the crow flies," an Earthsider might have put it—but the People have another expression which states the identical notion.

Alcyonius Nodus would afford them shelter and, probably, food, as the crumbling ancient cliffs of the mesa provide shelter for other life forms beside man.

Whether they could find water there, though, that was another question.

Had they dared ride due south, they could have found water at Nodus Laocontis, the old canal which once served to irrigate the gardens of Yeolarn.

Or they could have ridden southwest, into Nilosyrtis, an even greater canal which had similarly served the old, abandoned city near whose ruins the modern colony of Syrtis Port was built.

But these routes were too dangerous, as either would bring them within dangerous proximity to Yeolarn. And the two canals were more than twice as far away as Alcyonius.

So they rode on towards the Pole and the barren lands in the west.

Whether they would ever get there was another question and one which only time could answer.

## 5. The Cliff Dragon

RYKER HAD KNOWN from the first that there was something unusual about his three companions.

Their strangeness did not lie entirely in Valarda's uncanny golden eyes. Neither did it reside in the half-erased Clan tatoo on the boy's breast.

During the two days it took them to reach the mesa, he pieced the parts of the puzzle together and was able to put it into words.

*They did not act like Martians.*

The difference was subtle, not blatant. It took intuition to notice it. But Ryker noticed it.

In the first place, why were they willing to let him go with them? The People hate Earthsiders with a virulent intensity hard to describe, but it was more than than just the xenophobia most provincials feel for outsiders. The *F'yagha* had raped their world from them, and left them homeless vagabonds wandering amid the wreckage of their own empire. By contrast, the Apaches and Cherokees and other subjugated aborigines of the Americas had been treated with courteous and chivalric generosity. The Conquistadores had left Montezuma with more dignity and power than the Earthsiders had left the Martians.

True, he had intervened to save them from the mob. But an ordinary native woman and her retinue, under the same circumstances, would have thanked him frostily, and left him to his own devices.

Valarda was no ordinary woman. This he knew by sheer gut-level instinct.

Nor was she a dancing girl. Ryker had mingled much with the People, an outcast from his own kind, and there were Low Clan women who danced naked before men. Whereas she had the daintiness and reserve of a princess.

Of course, even a princess can be left destitute, homeless and starving by whims of fortune. The difference is that a princess would *rather* starve than show her nakedness before men. And he would have staked his life on the fact that Valarda was highborn.

As for the old man, he too displayed marks of breeding and elegance. His features were delicately carved, and there was nobility in his high brow. When he spoke, which was seldom, his accent and vocabulary were those of a learned man, a priest or a scholar. And no itinerant musician for a dancing girl ever bore a name like his. "Melandron" was a High Clan name, and a very ancient sort of name, at that. The sort of name the Old Kings had in the hero legends and epics of the past.

As for the boy, he was just a boy. Nothing was mysterious about him, save for the marking above his heart.

Ryker was two days with them before he discovered they had a secret language.

He spoke the Tongue as well, he supposed, as any *F'yagha.* Which is to say, he could make himself understood in it, and could interpret what was said to him pretty well. But the language of Mars is old beyond telling, rich in allusions to literature and folklore and legendry, with whole vocabularies of rare or obsolete words. There was much of the Tongue he could not and did not know. But he could recognize the main regional accents used by the major Clans, and these three spoke with an accent he had never before heard.

40

When, towards evening on the second day out of Yeolarn, they came within sight of Alcyonius Nodus, Valarda and the old man halted their steeds and sat there in the saddle for a time, staring at the mesa with an emotion in their eyes he could not name.

And when they spoke softly to each other, it was in a language he did not understand.

And this was *very* strange.

The Martians have been civilized for so many ages, they long ago lost national divisions. For millions of years they have been one nation, and the one Tongue is spoken universally from pole to pole. If once upon a time they spoke several different national languages, it was so very long ago they have forgotten it, even in their myths.

And the language in which Melandron and the girl conversed was not the Tongue. Or if it was, it was a dialect so ancient, or so rare, or so sacred, he did not recognize it.

He filed the fact away for later thought.

But he was beginning to wonder to himself, and strongly, where these three had come from.

It was like they were from another world.

Or another age.


That night they slept in a cave in the mesa wall. The boy Kiki had gone dart hunting, and had brought back fat scarlet lizards whereon that night they feasted.

Ryker had gone out to help, but when he saw the boy clambering over the cliff face as agile as any monkey, he knew there was nothing he could do.

And dart hunting is a Martian sport at which Ryker's sort are hopelessly clumsy. The slim metal shafts, like miniature javelins, were too light for his musculature, and Ryker knew it. Earthlings are built by evolution to stand erect under the crushing gravity of their heavy planet; they have more strength than is required on Mars, where a man who would weigh one hundred fifty pounds back on Earth here weighs only fifty-seven.

So he watched with helpless admiration as the boy cast his slim glinting darts at the rock lizards. They flickered through the air like weightless beams of light, transfixed the wriggling scarlet reptiles with unerring accuracy; and that night they feasted on *ongga*-steak broiled over chemical fire in spice leaves.

And they drank deep, having found in the deep crevices of the cliff rich growth of pod lichen the Martians crush and drain for precious water.

Here they were safe, with food, shelter and even water for their needs. By now Ryker was certain they were not being followed. The shambling gait of a loper's splay-footed stride raises a plume of the talcum-fine sands of the Dustlands you can see for many miles. And there were no far, dusty plumes behind them on the dark skies.

Ryker had tried a few casual questions, had been answered by silence, and gave it up. You do not intrude upon the privacy of this fierce, proud, wary people with blundering queries. What they wish you to know, they impart unasked.

But why wouldn't Valarda or the old man or the boy tell him where they were from, or the name of their tribe?

Actually, there could be many reasons. They could easily be outlaws, fleeing from tribe justice, or exiles, cast out by their chief.

*Or the last remnants of a dying people.*

Odd how that thought popped into his head.

Odder still how his skin crept and his nape hairs tingled at the thought. It was as if his body recognized the truth before his mind had reason to believe it.

42

Still, there was no evidence.

He set it aside to think about later.

That night, very late—near dawn, it was—Ryker came fully awake all of a sudden, as if some sixth sense warned him of danger.

Without the twitching of a single muscle, without changing the slow, deep rhythm of his breathing, did he give notice of his awakening. But with slitted eyes he searched the black gloom for a sign of difference.

A faint green glow from the residue in the fire pan was the only illumination that pierced the inky darkness of the cave. That, and a dim, blue-white glimmer from the thronging stars.

Nothing moved in the darkness, and no sound broke the stillness. He levered himself up on one arm, his other hand brushing his gun butt. There lay his companions bundled in their cloaks, spaced around the fire. Nor was there anything in the cave.

But something was wrong, he knew. He searched the green-lit gloom again—and then he saw it.

The girl was not there.

Her cloak and furs lay neatly arranged in the place she had selected for herself, but the place was empty.

Soundlessly as a cat, Ryker rose to his feet and padded to the mouth of the cave. Peering out, he saw her crouched in a huddle on the stone ledge. Cold blue starfire shone from her naked shoulders, caught and dazzled in her silken hair, and glowed upon the soft rondures of her bare breasts.

Ryker caught his breath at the loveliness of Valarda, nude in the starlight.

He must have made some slight sound—perhaps the

43

scuff of his boot leather rasping against dry stone—for she turned and saw him. And he saw that she had been weeping, for starfire glittered in her tear-wet lashes like tiny gems.

In the star sheen her perfect breasts were coppery silver above, polished ebony beneath. He had one swift, breathtaking look at her nakedness. Then she shook forward the black wings of her long hair, veiling from him the temptation of her tawny flesh.

And her face—open, vulnerable, soft lips atremble, some strange, heart-deep sorrow visible in her wet eyes—went hard and proud and cold. It was as if she had, in an instant, donned a lifeless mask; her eyes were frozen now, aloof, with the hauteur of a princess whose privacy a boor has blundered into.

He cursed himself for letting her discover him watching from the shadows like some panting voyeur. He opened his mouth to make some fumbling apology for intruding upon her privacy—and then, very suddenly, they were both of them too busy for words.

A terrible shape, black as night, edged with star jewels where the dim light caught its scales, clambered up over the brink of the ledge.

The *slioth* was a cliff scavenger, found commonly in these cliffs and mesas, which was accustomed to devouring the bodies of dead things. It did not usually prey upon the living, but—after all—meat is meat, and even the cliff dragon likes a hot, fresh meal at times.

For a split second it paused, clinging there by the suction pads on its six, hook-clawed feet. Then it slithered up and over the ledge and came at them, eyes burning like lamps of green phosphor, filled with a mindless, ravening hunger.

The girl sprang for the safety of the cave but Ryker was

in her way. She stumbled against him and went down on her knees and he tried to interpose his body between the lizard and the girl. One hooked paw raked him from throat to navel and he staggered back, until he stood flat against the wall of the cliff.

Miraculously, he was unharmed. The tough, insulated synthetic of his thermal suit had been built to keep in his bodyheat. It had never been designed to resist the terrible, razory claws of the *slioth* or its distant cousin, the dreaded sandcat of the Dustlands. But it was strong enough to keep those steely hooks from his flesh, although the fabric was slit open from neck to waist.

The lizard reared up, hissed like a steam whistle, and reached for them with three of its mailed limbs. Blood thundering in his ears like pounding surf, Ryker fumbled with numb, clumsy fingers for the gun which lay holstered against his thigh.

He half-drew it, and then, suddenly, the girl was in his arms, all of her cool, sweetly-rounded nakedness pressed against his own bared torso, her slim arms locked around his neck, making his draw awkward.

He cursed in harsh, senseless gutturals, swivelled to one side, and fired as the huge reptile loomed up, casting its black shadow over them.

In the inky gloom, the bolt of electric flame was brighter than many suns.

The cliff dragon was armored in leathery hide, and mailed with tough overlapping plates of horny chitin, like a lobster's shell. But the gun was set for a needle beam, and the sizzling ray lasered through the body of the beast and spurted from its back—bright, diffuse flame intermixed with gobbets of meat and thick, splattering gore.

The *slioth* squalled deafeningly. It fell backwards off

the ledge and, a moment later, they heard it thud against the rock-strewn slopes below.

The blaze of afterimages wavered before his eyes, blotting out everything but the pale, wide-eyed face the girl lifted to his. Where the soft roundness of her tender breast was pressed against his bare skin, he felt the thudding of her heart, and she felt his own heartbeat like an echo of hers.

She trembled in his arms, and he soothed her with strong, rough hands that were curiously gentle.

And then he kissed her, a tender probing kiss that went on and on as if their lips had grown together into one mouth. And she did not draw away until they both had to breathe.

She withdrew her body from his own then, and went into the cave, not looking at him, and left him there, stiffly leaning against the cliff, his chest and arms and mouth still tingling with the warmth of her and with the sweetness of her.

The boy and the old man stood, both naked, both saying nothing, both staring with wide, frightened eyes. The reek of burnt dragon meat was thick and sour on the dry, cold air.

He holstered his gun and stooped, entering the cave again. Valarda was curled up in her blankets, her back turned towards him so that he could not see her face.

No one said anything.

Ryker returned to his fur cloak and pretended to sleep.

But he lay awake for hours staring into the green-lit gloom, remembering the silken softness of her body against his own, and the honey sweetness of her mouth under his kiss.

# II
## *The Caravan Road*

## 6. The Oasis Town

DAWN HAD LIT the cave-roof with its pale luminance before Ryker got back to sleep, and when at last the others roused him it was near midday.

He went out to check on their lopers, and was surprised to find them unmolested. They had tethered the beasts at the foot of the cliff wall of the mesa, some distance up a narrow ravine where they could feed on the rock lichens and podweed. The *slioth* had not investigated the ravine, apparently.

As for the cliff dragon, its body was gone. Either the bolt from Ryker's power gun had not slain it outright, and it had dragged itself off to its lair, or its fellow scavengers had carried it away to feast in private.

Ryker thought it likely the beast had limped away on its own. Such reptiles are notoriously hard to kill, having brains so small it takes them hours to realize they are dead—an old hunting joke—and two hearts.

Nobody spoke over breakfast. And there was utterly no reference made to last night. It was as if none of it had even happened. Valarda did not meet his eyes, and served his meal with a cool reserve.

Ryker was just as glad. The embrace, the kiss, they had been one of those things and meant nothing. And he was in a surly, taciturn mood and felt little like conversation. The little imp, Kiki, however, had a twinkle of mischief in his green eyes as the boy demurely asked how he had slept.

They rode on that day, due west, following the curve of the meridian.

There had been some discussion about this, but not much. The girl informed him that they wished to reach the oasis of Yhakhah, where it was their intention to join a caravan traveling north.

This oasis town—actually, little more than a more-or-less permanent camp—stood at the northernmost terminus of the old waterway called Nilosyrtis, at the southern tip of the Casius Plateau. Now, it was the most logical place to go from where they were, perhaps; but Ryker still wondered why Valarda wished to venture into those parts. No matter what she had said to him, it simply could not be true that they wanted to travel north from that point. For north lay nothing: the barren cliff wall of the Casius, the bleak and uninhabited tableland itself, and then endless leagues of empty desert which stretched clear to the pole.

There was no city or encampment of the People north of Yhakhah. So where was she going?

There was more to all of this than met the eye, he knew. But he was in this, now, up to his neck. And there wasn't much else for him to do but go along, if only for the ride.

All that day they skirted the soaring cliff wall of the great mesa, riding west, carrying as much food and water as they could store. From time to time, Ryker eyed it curiously. The mesa meant something to Valarda and her old grandsire—if that is all he was. The Earthling recalled the curious emotion with which they had viewed it the previous evening. They had seemed—what?—appalled?, crestfallen?, saddened?

Now, why should that be? The mesa of Alcyonius Nodus was as it had ever been, a barren tableland of dead, sterile rock. And it had been thus for millions of years, surely, or anyway since the great oceans of prehistoric

Mars began to dry up. Once, perhaps , it had been a broad and fertile island, against whose cliffy shores the lost oceans had burst in shattering spray. But that was long ago.

They rode west, then north awhile until the mighty wall of the great pleateau darkened the horizon to the north. Reaching the foot of the plateau, they skirted it, riding west until sundown, and slept that night in the mouth of one of the innumerable ravines into which the cliffs of Casius were cloven.

The following day they caught their first glimpse of the broad Nilosyrtis. Once this canal had been a mighty river, perhaps, flowing down into the lowlands from the mountainous heights of Casius, and watering the Old City which stood at the northern extremity of that huge peninsula now called Syrtis Major. Now it was only a level plain covered with knee-high vegetation, weirdly blue.

When Mars began to dry up as the free water vapor in its atmosphere escaped in ever-dwindling amounts into space, the crust of the planet had shrunk and cracked, forming a network of long, geometrical lesions in the surface. Into these titanic ravines the shrinking oceans, or what was left of them, had drained. And over succeeding ages the Martian vegetation, adapting to ever-dwindling supplies of moisture, had taken root along these fissures, forming thick belts of hardy growths whose root systems delved down for miles into the pockets of moisture trapped within the bowels of the planet.

It was these broad strips of fertile vegetation the Earth astronomers had mistaken for artificial waterways. Only some of them, like Nilosyrtis, had once been the beds of primordial rivers, and only a very few showed any signs of having been engineered by human hands. While it was now thought that a few of the old canals had actually been

51

"mined" for water with immense rigs which had probably resembled the oilwells of Texas and Oklahoma, most of them were natural phenomena, and none of them bore even the slightest resemblance to the super Venetian canals which had webbed the planet from pole to pole in the imagination of Earthsider astronomers and fiction writers two centuries ago.

But here there was, truly, a source of water. For the low, rubbery, bright blue plants were a tough and hardy species whose leathery leaves and stems stored precious moisture hoisted drop by drop from whatever was left of the lost oceans at the planet's core. Here was both food and drink for man and beast, and a safe road they could follow to Yhakhah.

They rode into the old town at sundown and took rooms at an inn whose walls had already been ancient before the glaciers retreated from Europe, or the English Channel was born, or the first man made friends with the first dog.

There were a dozen of these oasis towns scattered over the face of Mars, and here all enmity was held in strict abeyance. Clan war or tribal feud or private vengeance were unknown. For towns such as Yhakhah were under Water Truce; here all men were as brothers banded together against a universal enemy, which was grim and hostile Nature herself. Here even the *F'yagha* could come without fear of danger. Here even the priests who had hunted Valarda would be powerless to harm her. (And Ryker wondered if they were still hunting her—and now him.)

And here she masked her eyes again, before they entered the town.

Ryker wished he knew more about the folklore of the People. Perhaps golden eyes, which he knew to be rare, were thought unlucky, or a stigma of witchcraft. Crossed eyes were once so regarded back on Earth, centuries ago, he knew—the origin of the "Evil Eye" of legend.

At any rate, she masked her own as they came riding into Yhakhah.

It was old, that town. The low wall around it, and parts of the buildings, showed that originally it had been built of huge blocks of the pale golden marble mined from the worn, low hills of Mars. The tooth of Time does not bite deep upon such dense stone, and they rode through pillared gates and down a long arcade of marble columns that had stood a million years or more, and still looked new and fresh, as if carried hither from the quarries only yesterday.

But the buildings had worn less well, and many of their walls had fallen and been patched together with the clay brick the Martians somehow manufacture on a desert world where water is more precious than rubies, and a lot scarcer. They were low roofed, the buildings, hunched and blear windowed, built every which way, in a tangle of meandering, narrow streets and dark alleys choked with refuse.

It was not pretty. But the patina of age had mellowed it and softened its harsh lines and enriched the dim colors of it, until in a way it was beautiful, in the way a very old woman can be beautiful: it had character.

The dim gold of the ancient marble, the dusty redbrown of the brickwork, the tawny lucency of the horn-paned windows, blended with the rich umber of the beaten soil, and the copper and ochre of the Dustlands that ringed it in.

Two, perhaps three, caravans were assembling in Yhakhah when they rode in under an evening sky of dusky crimson, or were resting here for the next leg of a long, slow journey that might carry them halfway around this world. The wineshops were roaring with song and odorous with cooked meats; drunken men lounged about or brawled or jested, lean, rangy men, caravan guards for the most part, half outlaw, with the look of wolves about them.

Slatternly oasis women loitered in doorways, or called hoarse, obscene invitations from windows. Naked urchins played in the streets or stood, sucking dirty thumbs, staring owlishly as they rode by.

Ryker had donned a hooded cloak, drawn close to hide his inches and his face. In a pinch he could pass for a warrior of the People. He had done it before and played the part now to perfection, swaggering when he had dismounted in the innyard, hooking his thumbs in his leather belt, which was worn over the kaftanlike cloak, drawn close to conceal the thermalsuit which would have revealed him at a glance as an Outworlder. Earthsiders could come and go with impunity here, true, but there was no point in calling attention to themselves. There might be eyes, even here, alert for a dancing girl, an old man and a child, who were accompanied by an Earthman.

Four of the first inns they tried were filled to capacity, but the fifth could house them. The surly innkeeper grudgingly informed Melandron one attic room was free. They must all sleep together, but they had done it before, in the cave, and could do it now.

Again, Ryker could not help but notice how Valarda held herself aloof, like a princess, and let her grandsire engage a room for them, and hire an oasis woman to prepare and serve their meals. He wondered about it to himself. On Mars, as in the desert countries back on Earth, youth abases itself before age. And if old Melandron was indeed her grandfather, as she had said he was, it should have been Valarda who performed these tasks, while the old man sunned himself in the yard, accepting wine with dignity.

But she treated him more like a retainer, and he deferred to her as he would to a queen.

They were weary from the long day's journey, and said little; and besides, the old witch of an oasis woman was there, cooking the meat over a hibachilike pot suspended over a pan of green chemical fire, and it would not do to discuss their business before a stranger.

The woman was needed because it was traditional, and they took the evening meal in the little garret, for the Martians do not customarily eat together in the common room with strangers, save at certain feasts.

After the meal, when the woman left, the old man left them at wine and went forth into the town to speak to the caravan men. Ryker would have done this, but Melandron curtly bade him tend Valarda, and there was nothing else for him to do but acquiesce.

She turned her eyes to him once, then, and looked into his own for virtually the first time since they had shared that kiss together under the starlight.

And at what he saw in the mysterious golden eyes of the dancing girl he had rescued from the mob in Yeolarn, Ryker felt a weight lift from his heart, and the blood sang within his veins, and there was no need for him to drink wine, for he was already drunk.

For the strange light that shone in her eyes when she looked at him he thought he knew. He had seen that light once before in the eyes of a woman, and it was like the glow that glimmers in Paradise.

# 7. The Jest of Kiki

WHILE THE PEOPLE only feast together in family groups or during certain festivities, it is traditional for them to drink together, rather than apart. And this was particularly true in towns like Yhakhah which are under Water Truce, for technically the Truce does not include travelers until they have drunk water and wine in common with strangers. It was the only form of water-sharing which does not place the Martian equivalent of blood-brotherhood upon two chance-met travelers, yet the obligation to hold the Truce is somewhat similar. And woe to him who breaks it.

Thus, although they were weary from the day's travel, they went down into the common room to drink with the caravan men, and to listen to the latest gossip. The relayer of this was a scrawny, bright-eyed little man with a comic puckered mouth and a nubbin of a nose, called a Juhangir. The Juhangir is the People's version of a medieval troubadour, itinerant clown, juggler and entertainer, all rolled into one in an amalgam uniquely Martian.

Between snatches of song and sketches of comic patter, the Juhangir relays the latest news and gossip, some of it months, even years, old, gathered by him during his lifelong, endless journey from town to town, city to city, camp to camp.

The Martians have no daily newsfax or stereovision commentators, they have only the wandering gossip mongerers they call Juhangir.

This particular clown, a little man named Goro, had

gathered his gossip in many far places, but had—Ryker was sincerely relieved to find out—heard naught of the latest events in Yeolarn. The big Outlander had tensed himself for the bad news that a *zhaggua* (whatever that meant to the People) had nearly been torn apart by a mob in Yeolarn, until a *F'yagh* rescued her, killing a priest with his power-guns.

Ryker breathed a sigh of relief when Goro finished, collected a few coins from the audience, and bowed himself away to his cubby. If gossip of their adventures had already reached Yhakhah, it could have been bad for them.

For there were priests here, even here.

After the skinny-shanked clown was through, a dancing girl came on. She looked hardly more than twelve or thirteen, her breasts scarcely budded, and she danced with coltish grace, but with none of the breathtaking artistry of Valarda. Her dance was frankly obscene, a naked wriggling invitation, and she simpered and giggled while undulating her bare tummy and loins before the grinning men. It was a disgusting thing to see, thought Ryker, although he was no prude and once he might have found it crudely exciting.

If they needed to replenish their dwindling store of coins here in Yhakhah, he thought to himself, Valarda could earn a fortune. The awkward nymphet barely wrung enough from her audience to buy a bauble, and went off to her grubby pallet accompanied by a leering, swaggering lout who would pay her scarcely more for a more intimate form of entertainment.

The room was large and long and low ceilinged, walled and roofed with stone, and floored with ancient, subtly colored tiles most likely thieved from one of the Dead Cities. It had a carved stone fireplace at one end, its

57

groined and arched roof was supported by stone columns, and in most ways it resembled the wineshop of Kammu Jha back in Yeolarn, where Ryker had first seen Valarda. But here, the walls opened off into small cubbyholes like dog kennels, and probably every bit as dirty and as odorous, where women or nubile girls like the one who had danced, or even boys—as the caravan men were not particularly fastidious about such pleasures—could be hired for immemorial purposes.

After the nymphet went out with her night's lover, Melandron returned to have wine with them. The old man proudly related his news: he had found a place for them in the train of a merchant who would depart for the north at midday tomorrow. He had spoken to the men in the bazaar, he told them, and only one of the caravans in town was heading north, and that was under the leadership of a merchant princeling known as N'kyha Houm of Bakrah.

Bakrah was a city of the People far to the south, Ryker knew, one of the few of the ancient metropolises of Mars which was still inhabited. The Prince of Bakrah was named Zarouk. He was more of a robber baron than a High Clan prince, he had an unsavory reputation.

"What payment did this Houm require, grandfather?" asked Valarda.

The old man dropped his eyes and drew a squiggly line with the tip of his forefinger in wet wine on the stone tabletop. Reluctantly, he named a sum. It was more than they possessed, Ryker realized, and he harshly said as much. For they had paid out , most of their trade money, including the few coins in his pocket, for their room and meal and wine.

Melandron made no reply, and continued to avoid their eyes. Kiki giggled maliciously, kicking his bare heels against the bench.

"*I* know!" the boy chirped. "He said you would dance naked for the men, lady!" He seemed to find the thought delicious, and shot a meaningful glance at Ryker, who was glowering at the notion.

Melandron hesitantly admitted that it was so.

Valarda said nothing for a moment, her masked features cold. Then she asked, tartly, "And did you promise I would share a cloak with this Houm, as well, old dodderer?"

"Of course not, my granddaughter," the old man said reprovingly.

"I thank the gods for that favor, if for naught else," she remarked. "Come, it is time to sleep."

They went up to their garret without speaking further.

Ryker found it difficult to get to sleep that night. He lay awake staring at the ceiling, thinking of Valarda.

That long look she had given him, the thing he thought he had read in her luminous golden eyes: was he right?

Was it a promise? Or was it, perhaps, an—invitation?

His mouth went dry at the thought.

She lay wrapped in her cloak, only a little ways apart from where he was stretched out, but he could not see her. The garret room was small and crowded, affording them no privacy. So he and the boy had strung lines up and draped blankets over them, effectively dividing the chamber into four tiny cubicles.

His loins ached at the thought of her nearness, at the memory of that slim, sinuous body pressed tight against his own, at the remembrance of the sweetness of her luscious mouth.

Suddenly—silently—the blanket wall was twitched aside, and Ryker caught a glimpse of a slender naked body entering his sleeping place.

He gasped and half-rose. In the next instant warm, supple limbs twined about him, pressing him down, and a mouth was upon his own. He returned the kiss avidly, hungrily, his hands gliding down a curved back to slim thighs, his heart drumming.

Then he froze incredulously, scarce daring to think.

He caught slim shoulders, pried the body from his own, and slid his hands up between them.

Instead of soft, yielding roundness, he touched the smooth, hard breast of a boy.

Roaring a furious oath in a voice half-strangled with fury, he jerked free and pulled away.

"You little imp!" he yelled, "I'll tan your bottom for you, if I ever get my hands on you!"

Doubled over with crowing laughter, Kiki scrambled from the cubicle, pausing momentarily at the part in the curtains to dart a mischievous, green-eyed glance at the contorted, crimsoning face of the outraged Earthling.

Then, with an impudent wiggle of his bare bottom, the grinning boy was gone.

His fury subsiding, Ryker sank back. Then it struck him funny in a sour way, and he grimaced, chuckling. The little rascal!—and he had taken it for granted that slim, vibrant body, bare against his own, was Valarda! And that eager, voluptuous mouth—

He scrubbed the back of his hand against his lips furiously. Maybe it served him right for thinking the dancer could go for a hairy, hulking Outworlder like himself.

But he resolved to get even with Kiki somehow. The urchin would bait him mercilessly for days over the success of his jest, otherwise.


Houm was a fat, merry man with a greasy, obsequious smile which contrasted curiously with his lordly ways. His fawning smiles, however, reached no further than his lips, and his small, slitted eyes were shrewd and coldly calculating.

He affected princely raiment and seemed forever to be stuffing sweetmeats in his mouth. And he wore altogether too many rings on his pudgy fingers for Ryker's liking.

Ryker did not like the man. Neither did he entirely trust him.

For his own part, though, the merchant from Bakrah seemed eager to have them ride north with his caravan, and was happy to have so stalwart a warrior as Ryker to join his outriders. These were needed to guard the caravan against the possibility of marauders, for danger was always present in these northerly regions, which were far beyond the territories protected by the rule of the great High Clan princes. Outlaw bands might well lurk among the ravines of Casius to ambush passersby; and even slavers were not unknown north of Syrtis.

One more outrider was a welcome addition to Houm's troop of guards, even if he was a *F'yagh*. The fat man measured Ryker's tall, brawny frame, noted his hard, suspicious eyes and the way the tips of his calloused fingers never strayed far from the well-worn gun butts, and nodded approvingly.

The chief of Houm's guards was a rangy, wolfish warrior called Xinga. If anything, the desert rider looked even more of a ruffian than the lean, leathery men he commanded. But he looked capable enough. Xinga assigned Ryker to the right guard of the caravan's front, and Ryker gave a surly nod of assent. He did not like to be separated from Valarda, but had no say in the matter.

At least, his assignment would keep him out of reach of Kiki's knowing grins for the day. The boy had burst into fits of giggling every time he saw the grumpy expression on Ryker's face, and the big man had flushed crimson each time this happened, and yearned to up-end the child and apply the palm of his strong right hand to that bare and impudent little bottom.

The caravan departed from the oasis town of Yhakhah at midday as scheduled, and headed north along the old stone-paved way which bordered the Nilosyrtis.

For some time they rode with the broad acres of blue, rubbery-leafed plants to their right hand, and the highlands of Casius dead ahead, marching across the world from horizon to horizon like a wall built by captive titans.

There were some twenty-five covered wains comprising the main body of the caravan, and they looked for all the world like pictures of the ancient covered wagons the pioneers had used to cross the western plains Ryker had seen in history tapes. The wains were not made of wood, however, since nothing resembling a tree is to be found on water-poor, oxygen-starved Mars. Instead, the capacious, high-sided wagons were constructed from panels of thick, tar soaked canvas, fastened together with metal joints and hinges. The People weave this cloth from plant fibre, and it is remarkably tough and durable. These wains were loaded with merchandise: wines from the south in ceramic casks; liqueurs, syrups, dyes and perfumes; bolts of rare silks, colored cloths, and the gorgeous tapestries and carpets of Shiaze, Yukara and Diome.

Houm carried carven ivory and jewelry and tradeware of copper and bronze as well, for gifts to the northern chieftains of the towns and encampments he planned to visit.

The guards were a rough lot, clad in tunics and jerkins of black leather with long cloaks of fur. Some wore helmets of metal, others high hats of black felt, or turbanlike headdresses of colored cloth. Hoops of gold dangled in their earlobes, and their leather trappings were adorned with small plaques of precious metal and jewelled ornaments.

This ostentatious display was not a display occasioned by vanity, but a simple precaution. There are no banking institutions on Mars, or at least none that will deal with the natives, and no safety deposit boxes, either. The People either carry their wealth on their person, or conceal it in their homes, or bury it in the dead sea bottoms or on the highlands far from other men, returning to dig it up months or even years later. This being so, treasure maps, generally spurious ones, are easy to buy on Mars, but are purchased mainly by the gullible. The People need no maps to find their hidden caches. Nature has given them an innate sense of location which is uncannily accurate.

Ryker took a lot of hazing from the guards, who disliked having one of the despised *F'yagha* amongst them. He endured their insults in grim silence, but when the punishment became tentatively physical it was a different matter. Despite the fact that he wore power-guns, while they were only armed with swords, dirks, spears and targes, they dared to lay their hands upon him.

These weapons, he knew, were mostly for show. Their real weapons hung over their shoulders—slim, hollow, long black tubes which were used like blowguns, and thin flat quivers of needlelike darts used in the tubes, and poison tipped, as like as not. Guns were no deadlier than those long black tubes, he knew, and he would lose face with the men if he went for them.

Instead he waded in with balled fists and battered his chief tormentor to his knees in a few seconds. It was not hard, as the People have no knowledge of the fine art of the prize ring. His opponent, a long-legged fellow called

Raith, climbed painfully to his feet and swayed awhile, fingering a loose tooth and spitting blood. Then he came over to Ryker, slapped him on the shoulder a time or two, and called him a dirty name, grinning.

Ryker grinned back, and called Raith by an even deadlier insult. The other men hooted, slapped their thighs, and relaxed. And he was accepted—for a time, at least.

That night they made camp under the jewelled skies, having drawn the wagons into a huge ring. Green flames lit the gloom, meat sizzled on spits, and leathern bottles of fire-hearted wine were passed from hand to hand. After drinking, they drew apart to eat in private.

Then, posting guards about the perimeter of the circle, they bedded down in their cloaks and slept.

Ryker, as a very junior newcomer, had the first watch, as did Raith, in punishment for letting himself be beaten by a mere *F'yagh.* He leaned on his tall spear, and watched the stars wheel across the sky, and thought of Valarda. His need for her was like an ache deep in his groin.

He had been a long time without a woman. And men like him have strong need for women, as other men need wealth or fame or power.

That night, his watch done, he slept deep and there were no dreams.

# 8. The Dead City

BY THE FOLLOWING afternoon they reached the foothills of the Casius. The vast plateau obliterated half the sky, cutting the world in two. Once, perhaps, it had been a small northern continent near the Pole, like Greenland back on Earth. Now it was only a bleak, barren expanse of stony desolation, although pod-lichen lived in the clefts, and rock lizards, too, and probably *slioths.*

Here they were forced to take refuge from a duststorm, one of the rare phenomena which occur often enough to remind visitors from Earth, gasping on the thin, dry air, that Mars truly does have an atmosphere, and even winds at times.

Like sandstorms in the desert countries back home, Ryker knew, the airborne deluge of whirling dust can be, and often is, deadly. The talcum-soft powder seeps through cloth with ease, and works into your lungs, bringing the coughing sickness they call *yagh.*

He had seen a man die of it once, and it was not a nice thing to watch. Houm evidently felt the same way, and hastily guided the caravan off course to the west as soon as the storm showed visibly, a sooty smudge against the sky.

*Why west?* Ryker wondered silently to himself. He would have thought it best to have driven north, to the cliff wall of the great plateau, where surely they could take refuge from the whirlwind in one of the deep, narrow ravines that cleft the wall of stone asunder in a thousand places. But Houm seemed to know where he was going, and before long Ryker got a surprise.

As they urged their lopers across the desert with all the speed they could coax or coerce or cudgel out of the troublesome creatures, riding before the wind which yammered in their ears like a screeching devil horde, they came upon a city in the sands, lost and forgotten for ages.

It was one of the Dead Cities, Ryker knew. There were many such as this scattered across the dusty face of Mars, abandoned as the wells ran dry or the inhabitants dwindled to a handful. It was just that he had not known there was one this far north, this near the Pole. For they were in the Dustlands of Meroe, near the narrow isthmus which connects Casius and its sister plateau to the west, Boreosyrtis. And the city was only some thirty-eight miles or so south of the maximum winter limit of the polar ice.

Which meant the city was . . . *old*.

A chill ran tingling up Ryker's spine at the sight of it, the fallen walls mouldering in deep-drifted dust, the riven minarets which leaned and some of which lay fallen, broken into sections, *and the long stone quays, crusted with fossilized barnacles,* which thrust out from the dockfront into the dead, empty Dustlands.

This city had been already old before the oceans died.

Ryker gaped, and muttered a dazed oath. A city *that* old should have been one of the wonders of Mars, famed afar, crawling with tourists, rifled by three generations of archaeologists. And he hadn't even known it was there!

But Houm had, evidently.

They entered the lost city well ahead of the duststorm, and sought refuge in a large domed structure whose walls were still intact and where, presumably, they would be safe from the dangers of the tempest. They stabled the wains and beasts within an inner court, high walled and secure enough.

Houm acted as if he knew this place well, and that did not seem odd to Ryker until he got a good look at the interior of the domed citadel. Its furnishings were intact, although greatly worn by age and neglect. The tapestries and wall hangings were ragged and their brilliant hues were dimmed by the ages, but Ryker knew enough about such things to guess that they would still bring a rich price in the back alleys of Syrtis. And the low couches and tabourets, inlaid with carven plaques of mellow ivory, glistening purple winestone and rare carnelian, which stood undecayed by time and unmolested by men, were fabulous antiques.

Why, then, had not Houm looted the dead city long ago, since he must have been here before? It was curious. It was more than curious, it was suspicious.

But, to be honest, Ryker didn't know what to be suspicious about.

For the present, he resolved to keep his mouth shut and to act unconcerned. But he grimly vowed to keep his eyes and ears open.

The storm was soon over. In fact, it never struck at all, but faded as its furies ebbed and the winds died, the shrieking whorls of deathly dust subsiding, dissipating before they even reached the city.

At its first appearance, Ryker had half a notion that it was too low on the horizon to be one of those deathstorms that rage for days on end and bury men and beasts alive. But Houm seemed fearful and ordered them to run for cover, and Houm knew this part of the North Country better than did Ryker, so the Earthling forgot about his first intimation until it was proven accurate.

Odd, then, that Houm had panicked so, since even Ryker, a stranger to these parts, had guessed from the first that the storm would subside as swiftly as it had arisen. It was almost as if the fat, beringed merchant had seized upon a convenient pretext for diverting the caravan from its announced route and entering the lost city.

And, now that they were here, Houm seemed in no particular hurry to depart. In fact, it seemed to Ryker as if the clever little trader was seeking every excuse that came to mind to linger here a bit longer.

First he demanded the wainmasters inspect their wheels and grease the axels and gears, as if he feared the dust had clogged them. This made good sense, for if one or another of the wagons had broken down in the middle of the desert of Meroe, it would have been a costly, even a dangerous hindrance. But the wainmasters reported no accumulation of dust.

Whereupon Houm found one reason after another for lingering overnight in the town. The beasts, he said, were too wearied to reach the isthmus before nightfall; and it was better they camp here now, than be caught short on time in the Dustlands. It all seemed very suspicious to Ryker.

The upper floor of the citadel was divided into many rooms, which were assigned for sleeping and eating. Kiki and Melandron and the girl were given one of them. Ryker joined them at the meal, being off-duty for a time.

And there was another strangeness he observed.

When they had taken their first look at the incredibly ancient town, Ryker had been struck with awe, and had stared about him with wonderment. He had chanced to notice the reaction of Valarda and her grandsire at the same moment, being near thier wain.

The emotions legible in thier wide eyes and stricken

features had puzzled him at the time. For they seemed struck dumb with shock and horror and with another emotion he could only name with the name of . . . *sorrow.*

Now, why should these ancient ruins, which had stood collapsed in this same state of advanced decay for millions of years, virtually unchanged in the dry, weatherless atmosphere of Mars, have caused them such consternation?

*It was almost as if they somehow remembered the city from an ancient time, when it was new and whole and beautiful.* . . .

But that was crazy, of course.

Over the meal, he could not help noticing how withdrawn and crestfallen the two seemed. They barely said a word and when they did it was to mutter in that unknown dialect of theirs whereof he was ignorant. But he read with deep sorrow the sadness and despair which were written in their faces, and it was a mystery to him. He sought an analogue for their strange sorrow and realized at length that it was akin to the tragic horror one would feel, seeing again an old friend you had not visited in years, to find him hideously wasted and aged by some horrible and hopeless disease.

Now, why in the world should the appearance of this ancient city affect them so strongly?

Ryker shook his head numbly, his wits baffled. There were too many mysteries here, and he didn't like it.

After the meal they went down into the great rotunda that was the main hall of the citadel, to share water and wine.

And here Valarda danced again.

Houm begged it of her, waving his wine goblet jovially, and the men grinned wolfishly, echoing his wish. Nor could Valarda deny them their request, for Houm had made this a condition for their joining his caravan, and her own grandsire had promised it on her behalf.

So, while the men drank another round, and old Melandron went into his pitch, praising her beauty and the grace and seductiveness of her body, in a sing-song voice—a ritual he had evidently repeated many times in many wineshops—Valarda retired to oil her body and dust it down with the glittering powder traditionally worn by one of her profession.

Ryker liked this little, but there was nothing he could do about it. The girl had not "shared a cloak" with him, which would have given him a proprietary right to refuse that she bare herself before the men. So he had to grin and endure it.

Little Kiki had gone back to their room to fetch down drum and pipe and begging bowl, so Ryker had nothing to do but sit and watch. And drink the strong, sour wine.

Valarda danced like the pure flame of a candle wavering in the wind, like a plume of golden desert dust floating before the breeze, and, as before, the room grew silent until all you could hear above the squeal of Kiki's pipe and the thump and pitter of the old man's drum was the hoarse breathing of men caught by the throat in the grip of desire.

She was very beautiful.

Her dance was a naked and wanton temptation, a thing of sheer lust, the quintessence of animal passion.

Ryker's throat was dry and his heart pounded painfully, and there was a throbbing in his head that was not caused by wine.

Her beauty was such that it clenched at his loins, and roused a male hunger within him. It was torture for him to see the allure of her nakedness, and to know that other men felt it, too.

70

Houm watched with his head tipped on one side and an amiable, avuncular smile on his fat face. But the hot glitter in his little eyes belied the kindly paternalism in his smile. It was the gleam of greed.

Two men sat with Houm on his carpeted pallet, and they were men that Ryker had not seen with the caravan before, and that was odd. One was tall and lean and curiously elegant, although wrapped in a disreputable cloak like a beggar. His features were hard, fierce, aquiline: there was breeding in them, and pride. The other man was small and hunched and spindle shanked, and he hid his face in the shadow of his hooded cloak. Ryker eyed them curiously, wondering where they had been hidden all this while. He could have sworn that he knew at sight every last member of the caravan, even the painted, pampered, simpering boy slave Houm kept apart for his own pleasure.

Finally he asked Raith about it. The tall guardsman sat next to him, and they had become good comrades ever since Ryker had knocked him down and ended the hazing.

"They're new," Raith shrugged.

"What do you mean, 'new'?"

The warrior shrugged, incuriously. "Came riding in an hour ago, when you were having meat. I was on guard and saw them. Old Houm was waiting for them, I think. At least, he seemed mighty relieved when they turned up, and glad to see them."

"Do you know who they are?" Ryker asked.

"I don't know the tall one," admitted Raith. "But the little fellow with him is a Juhangir . . ."

An alert, wary flame leaped up in Ryker's colorless eyes.

"Named Goro? The one who entertained back at Yhakhah?"

"That's the one."

Ryker said nothing, but now he was no longer curious. Now he was *afraid*.

It took him quite a while to get to sleep that night, with so many small, annoying mysteries on his mind. Finally he did manage to drift off, although his sleep was shallow and troubled by shadowy and ominous dreams.

An hour or so before dawn he came fully awake, suddenly, tingling all over with apprehension. Something had disturbed his light slumbers. But, what?

He threw back the fold of his cloak of furs and raised himself on one arm, looking around. The energy gun was ready in his hand.

But he saw nothing, nothing at all. The bare, empty room of the ancient citadel, rubbish in the corners, the faded hues of curious antique murals—naught else was visible in the dim green glow of chemical flame. The metal pan stood on the floor by the door, shedding its emerald illumination evenly over the room. By this night light, which the Martians leave burning when they sleep, believing that green light repels the night-wandering apparitions and vampiric demons of the dark which throng their old mythology, he saw nothing suspicious.

It was merely a superstition, of course, but a night light sometimes comes in handy. As now, for instance, Ryker could see that no one was there.

From beyond the half-open door he heard the distant mutter of men in the suites below, being awakened to replace the guards. From the courtyard beyond his unshuttered window, he heard the beasts stirring in their sleep, and the restless clatter of their splay-footed feet against the worn old tiles.

The early morning was so still that he could hear even these faint, far, familiar sounds.

What, then, had startled him into awakening so suddenly?

Then he felt the night-chill against his heart. And knew that his garments were disarranged—and not by him.

His thermals were held together by pressure seams, which could not easily be opened. But *something* had opened them, laying naked the flesh above his heart.

A dim premonition stirred within him, then.

For around his neck in a leather bag he wore the black seal he had found in the ancient tomb.

Now, why on Earth—or on Mars—would anybody be interested in *that?*

# 9. "ZHAGGUA!"

PERHAPS IT HAD not been anyone after the black seal at all, he reasoned to himself. For, after all, it still lay snug and safe in the little leather bag he wore suspended about his neck on a thong. To make certain of this, he opened the bag, took out the carven piece of heavy black crystallike stone and examined it closely by the green glow. Then he put it away.

Perhaps his thief in the night had simply been that—a thief. Thieves seek valuables—currency, coins, gems. And Ryker's pockets were bare of these things, God knew! He grinned sourly, shrugged, and lay back in the folds of his cloak, composing himself to snatch what little of the night was left before he must rise to the duties of the day.

But he had drunk deeply of the strong wine the night before, watching Valarda dance naked before the men, and the pressure of his kidneys goaded him reluctantly from the room to seek a privy.

There was a dry well in the courtyard where the *slidars* were tethered, he remembered. He headed downstairs for it. But at the head of the stairway he froze motionless, straining his ears, his gun out and ready.

There were men ascending the stairs, many men, moving with furtive stealth, keeping as quiet as was possible.

Ryker knew this by blind, unreasoning instinct. He had

been pursued and hunted in his time, and men walk in a different way when they are trying to creep up on someone without being seen or heard, than when they are just trying not to awaken their sleeping comrades.

He melted into the shadows then, and when the band of men reached the head of the stair he was nowhere to be seen.

It was out in the open at last. The time of lies and cunning wiles and impostures was over with. Whatever this thing really was, however ugly, it was about to reveal itself.

Dawn broke dim gold in the east, and the caravan was in an uproar. During the early morning a band of desert warriors had come riding into the dead city, bearing with them an Earthling captive. The presence of the captive, an old man with white hair, surprised no one. The surprise was that the warriors had ridden in without the alarm being sounded.

For Houm himself, and the two strangers who had shared his carpet with him at the drinking of wine last night, were dressed and awake and waiting at the gate to welcome the newcomers.

Word flew from mouth to mouth that the tall, hawk-faced stranger of the night before, who had watched Valarda dance with cold, searching, yet avid eyes, was Prince Zarouk himself, the desert marauder of the south of whom all had heard much, and little that was to their taste.

But further surprises were in store.

Down from the third story of the citadel came a band of Zarouk's tall, long-legged warriors, grinning wolfishly.

With them they bore three captives—the dancing girl, the old man, and that imp of a boy!

75

The three were dragged forth into the gold light of dawn, and it could be seen that their arms and wrists were bound behind their backs by tight leathern thongs. Seeing them, the Prince strode forward, a cold smile on his thin, bearded lips. Houm stood smirking, fingering his little queue of a goatee. Silence fell—tense, tight, expectant.

The girl's head was sunk upon her breast, the pale oval of her perfect face veiled beneath the black wings of her long hair.

Zarouk reached out and took her by the throat.

"Raise your head, slut!" he snarled. "Open your eyes, that all men may see you as you are, and may know the vile thing you be."

Valarda lifted her face into the light and looked upon the caravan men and the desert raiders with great golden eyes.

A shudder as of loathing ran through the crowd. And men began to speak a word, first in a whisper, then in a mutter, then and at last in a growling chant.

*"Zhaggua . . . Zhaggua . . . ZHAGGUA!"*

There was fear in their voices, aye, and contempt, and also hatred. They did not so much utter the despised name as spit it in her face like phlegm.

But Valarda neither flinched nor let the slightest flicker of emotion shadow her expression of pride and disdain. No haughty French aristocrat ever faced the guillotine during the Terror with such proud disdain, nor with such courage.

Zarouk chuckled, enjoying the drama of the moment. He showed his white teeth in a leering smile, and his eyes gloated on the three captives. He flung up his head in a bold gesture.

"What shall we do with this *zhaggua* and her pack?"

he cried. "Dmu, what says The Book? What is the end decreed most fitting for such vermin, and most pleasing to the Timeless Ones?"*

Forth from the throng of tall, robed desert warriors there came shuffling into view a small, old man with the shaven pate and silver ear-sigils of a native priest, his gaunt, bent, wasted form wrapped in dark, dusty robes, his hands tucked into his voluminous sleeves.

The men made way for him a bit uneasily. Priests are respected on Mars, but not exactly loved. Few even of the devout feel comfortable in their presence. Perhaps they stand too close to the eternal mysteries of creation and judgment and doom, and the gates of life and death, for ordinary men to enjoy their company.

"The Death of the Slow Fire, lord Prince," the old priest said in a thin, quavering sing-song voice. And his rheumy, lusterless eyes brightened as he said this.

The men stood silent, glancing at each other. It was a slow, agonizing death the priest had named. The green, flaming chemical that lights the demon-frighting lamps falls drop by searing drop upon the writhing naked body of the condemned. These were rough, hard men, and they loathed Valarda's kind with an ancient loathing. But more than a few turned pale or looked away.

---

*"The Book" is what the People call the holy scriptures of their aeon-old religion, but of course they use their own language to name it. The "Timeless Ones" are the three gods of the Martian pantheon, believed forever sleeping in the underworld of Yhoom, which is beyond the reach of time or change. From this sleep they will arise on the Day of Doom, to judge the world and decide its ultimate destiny. For more on The Book, the Timeless Ones themselves, and Yhoom, see my novel *The Man Who Loved Mars,* published by Fawcett Gold Medal Books in 1973.

Houm, however, smiled and licked his thick lips. *And then the world changed with a crash.*

From nowhere a needle of incandescence flared. It sizzled before the very booted toes of Prince Zarouk, searing a black, smoking line between the desert chieftain and his captives. Almost before the fire-needle vanished, a voice from above rang out, hard and sharp as the crack of a whip.

*"Nobody moves!"*

A hundred eyes searched the upper works of the citadel and found him on the ledge.

Ryker with his guns out and ready, and the deadly fury of hell naked in his cold, ice-colored eyes.

They put a league of dust-desert between them and the dead city before Ryker dared let them slow their stride.

The lopers they had taken were their own, but were well rested from Houm's delay in the city, where he had evidently arrived earlier than convenient for Zarouk to meet him at their prearranged rendezvous. There were doubtless faster *slidars* to be found among the caravan beasts, but they were accustomed to these brutes.

They had ridden fast and hard and almost without words, not even words of thanks for the rescue Ryker had so brilliantly pulled off. But as they had mounted into the saddles back there in the courtyard, ringed about by silent men with eyes that spoke their hatred for them, Valarda had lifted her golden eyes to those of the Earthling for one long, searching look. Tears glistened in her silky lashes, and her soft red mouth had been tender, vulnerable, trembling with emotion.

He had grinned, saying nothing. Sometimes words can be unspoken, and yet heard clearly, and maybe this was one of those times.

For a bit of extra life insurance, Ryker suggested they take the long-legged desert prince with them, and also his pet priest, whose name turned out to be Dmu Dran. These two he had commanded bound with the same leathern thongs as had bound the wrists of the girl, the boy, and the old man.

The boy Kiki did the tying. And he did it with a vengeance, pulling the tough thongs tight and tighter still, even as Zarouk's henchmen had pulled them tight.

The old priest, sunk in apathy, his withered mask of a face dull eyed and vacant, did not wince—perhaps the lad had gone easy on his bonds. But Kiki had tied the desert prince tight indeed. Zarouk had not winced, either, and the tight-lipped silence and the curious dignity—even a sort of majesty—with which the maurauder accepted this sudden and unexpected reversal of fate won him Ryker's grudging but unspoken respect.

But if his tongue was silent, his eyes were eloquent and spoke volumes. They burned with hellfire, those amber eyes, and were as quick and alert and deadly as a snake's.

*This is a bad man to have for your enemy,* thought Ryker to himself, sourly, cursing the day he had ever gotten himself mixed up in this stinking mess. But if he hadn't, he would never have found Valarda . . . never have seen her dance . . . never have gazed deep into those unforgettable eyes of fluid gold . . . .

Still, Zarouk would make a deadly foe, he knew. The man was all fire and pride and ambition, stretched tight as a trigger and thirsty for blood. An unsettling, explosive amalgam of religious fanatic and something of the megalomaniac, he decided. Ryker didn't know just how he knew it, but he hadn't kept alive this long without being able to read men at a glance.

And he was seldom wrong. Not about men like Zarouk.

This was the sort of man who would follow you across the wide world, if you earned his hate. He would track you to the very doorstep of hell, to have his revenge.

So maybe it was best to have him at your side, Ryker had decided. Then, if his men break their sworn oath, and follow, or lay ambush, or attack, you can at least have the pleasure of taking him down to hell with you, with a yard of sword steel through his guts before you get the same through yours.

He hadn't thought to bring Houm along as well. He judged that the shrewd, greedy little merchant could be tempted and hired to flirt with danger for gold, but probably didn't give a damn for vengeance or religion or much of anything else, except perhaps the fat, giggling boy he kept as a pet.

And there is where Ryker made the worst mistake of his life.

They got a league and a little more into the northern parts of the Merope before the lopers died beneath them. They had been given a slow-acting poison, probably the night before. Maybe Houm figured that Ryker might have his wind up, and would spook easy, or be wary enough to try to make a break for freedom during the night. Or maybe one of his men had fed the poisoned food to the *slidars* when it became obvious, back in the courtyard, what his plans were.

It didn't matter. What mattered was that they were afoot now in the Dustlands and would have to walk all the way to wherever it was they were going, with a hundred desert warriors behind them, armed and mounted and hungry for revenge.

So they started walking. There wasn't anything else to do.

## 10. The Betrayal

THEY TRUDGED THROUGH the Dustlands of the northern Merope all the rest of that day, putting as much distance between themselves and Zarouk's desert hawks as could humanly be done.

It was hard going.

The dust was as fine and as soft as talcum powder, and in the light gravity of this world, where an Earthling weighs about one third what he would weigh back home, they raised the dust with every step. It clung to their robes, their furs, it coated their faces and worked its way into eyes and nostrils and the inside of their mouths. And there was nothing they could do about it but endure it.

The desert dust was so soft that men sank to their ankles in it, and, after a time, walking became sheer torture. It was like wading through foot-deep molasses. Every step of the way, the dust dragged against the pull of your muscles, until they ached as if hot needles were thrust into them.

There was no cure for this discomfort, either.

When after a time the old man, Melandron, fell to his knees and could go no further, Ryker knew that he had assumed the leadership of this unlucky expedition, and that from here on all of the hard decisions were up to him.

The old man feebly begged them to leave him and go on without him. Valarda said nothing; she bit her lip and veiled her gold eyes behind shadowy lashes. The boy Kiki was downcast and silent. His mischievous pranks and merry jests were a thing of the past now, for even his youthful ebullience and supple strength were worn and wearied.

Ryker gruffly bade the old man be silent, ignored his weak struggles, and picked him up in his arms. A flicker came and went swiftly in the eyes of Zarouk. Almost too swiftly for notice, the desert prince resumed his imperturbable, bland expression. But Ryker had seen that flicker, and realized that if he must carry Melandron his hands would not be free to go for his guns, if go for them he must.

He solved both problems easily, by making *Zarouk* carry the old man! The prince bit his lip, scowled, but did as he was told. Rather than cut his hands free, Ryker had him carry Valarda's grandsire piggyback.

They trudged on.

There was no water, only a little wine. This he rationed out in grudging sips. It was barely sufficient to wet parched, dust-covered lips, but it would have to do.

The old priest, Dmu Dran, did not weaken and have to be carried, and for this, at least, Ryker was grimly thankful. The priest was an enemy, and, even in the best of times, Ryker bore no love for priests—Martian or Earthsider—but he wasn't sure he had it in him to abandon the old man to die the slow death of dehydration.

Thank God he didn't have to make *that* decision. For, despite his age and seeming frailty, the fanatic seemed tireless as iron.

The cliffs that were the sides of the great plateau were ever before them, but never seemed to get any nearer. They danced and wavered in the tired vision of the travelers like some devilish mirage of the waste, and seemed in fact to recede into the distance the closer you came.

Ryker, who had the rudiments of an education, thought

of Tantalus and Ixion and Sisyphus, and of the torments invented for them by the gods. He grinned sourly; Mars could have taught a lesson or two to the Olympians, when it came to dreaming up tortures.

They plodded on, and every foot seemed like a mile, and every minute like an hour. Somehow they kept going.

At last they reached the foot of the plateau, which proved to be no illusion after all. Here they would have fallen to the ground to sleep where they fell, but Ryker drove them on with oaths and blows and curses.

He was made of granite, but even granite can crack and crumble. For a little while longer, though, he held strong.

He drove them into the mouth of a deep, narrow ravine, and made them follow it. They stumbled along on numb legs, dazed and mindless, like men who walked in their sleep. Between the tall, towering walls the ravine twisted and turned, but at its end the solid rock of the plateau was worn away in strata which could be climbed, although not easily.

It was like ascending a staircase built for giants, but they made it to the top of the plateau. And here he allowed them to rest and to make camp. Here he felt safe—safe enough, at any rate. He knew that the desert hawks would be following them. But he also knew there was no way for Zarouk's warriors to tell which of the ten thousand ravines into which the edge of the plateau was cloven was the one they had followed.

And from the edge of the cliff wall, by daylight, he could see for many miles, and spot the raiders on their trail.

He did not let Valarda make a fire. Fire can be seen far off in the black gloom of a Martian night. So they munched dry bread and devoured cold meat, huddled in their fur cloaks for warmth. They had each two mouthfuls of cold wine from the leather bottles, and it was Valarda who served them.

Ryker was bone weary by now, and so tired that his brain felt numb and dead as if his skull were stuffed with cotton, but he drove himself a bit further. There were two prisoners to tend to, and both were very dangerous and deadly enemies. But, after all, they too were men.

So he unbound their hands and stood by, his palms resting on his gun butts, watching while Zarouk and the aged priest chafed the blood back to their stiff limbs. He permitted them to relieve themselves a little ways from camp, then herded them back with the others, and bound their hands again, and their ankles, too, this time, and wrapped them in their cloaks for sleep.

Probably, he should have killed them or left them at the foot of the cliff to die in the night, but it was not in him to murder men in cold blood. So, cursing himself for his weakness, he let them live a while longer.

Then he slept. There was no strength left in him to stand guard all night. And, anyway, the wine had made him woozy and more than a little drunk. And he would need every atom of his strength to go on tomorrow.

He slept like a dead man. The deep, bottomless sleep of absolute exhaustion. And there were no dreams this time.

He had done all that a man could do. He had taken every precaution that was possible for a man of his fiber. The two captives he made sleep apart, with the others between them, to reduce the possibility that they might crawl together in the darkness and work each other's bonds free.

He had no fear of this. Zarouk and Dmu Dran were only men, and probably far wearier than he. They, too, would sleep deeply—as deeply as he.

Which is why he awoke sometime after sunrise, astonished to find his guns gone and his wrists tied behind him with leather thongs.

Ryker rolled over onto his back and peered around him with a cold horror in his heart and a sinking feeling deep in his guts at what he would see.

But instead of what he had feared, quite a different sight met his eyes.

"Surprised, scum?" Zarouk asked, in a voice like iron scraping against iron. "No man can trust a *zhaggua*. Now you have learned the truth of it, fool!"

Ryker stared. Valarda and Melandron and the boy Kiki were nowhere to be seen. They were gone. Gone, too, were their sleeping furs, and all the gear. And the food and drink they had carried off from the caravan encampment, and the weapons, too.

He rolled onto one side and sat up, painfully and stiffly, unable to believe the evidence of his senses.

The holsters strapped to his thighs were empty. They had taken his guns.

And then it came to him that one other thing was gone from him as well, an old, familiar weight he had worn over his heart for so long that he had become accustomed to the weight of it, and hardly felt it any more.

Now the very absence of that weight reminded him of it.

The ancient black seal he had carried in a little leather bag suspended about his throat by a thong was missing!

Bag, seal and thong they had stolen.

*And left him here to die.*

His heart contracted, became a cold, hard lump within his breast. And something within him died then. Something he had begun to feel for the girl with the golden eyes . . . something that was more than mere lust or mere desire . . . something that had begun in a hungry wanting, but had grown and flowered into something that was very close to love.

Dead, now, that emotion. Burnt to ashes in the fires of the fierce, hating fury that woke within him.

Zarouk saw it in the hard mask of his face and the deadly coldness of his slitted eyes, and laughed to see it. The old priest who lay across from him, hooded eyes fixed on nothing, must have felt it too, but said nothing. His heart was so charged with the venom of hatred there was no room for more.

Sometime in the night while he had lain in that deathlike sleep of utter weariness—or in the first light of dawn, perhaps—they had quietly awakened—Valarda and her old grandsire and the naked imp of a boy.

Stealthily and furtively, they had crept upon Ryker and thieved from him his power guns and the thing that lay above upon his heart in the little leather bag.

Then, gently and carefully, so as not to waken him, they had bound his wrists together so that he was helpless. Then they had gathered up their furs, and all the food and drink there was left, and stole away like the thieves they were.

Or maybe they hadn't been so gentle and so careful with him, after all. Maybe they hadn't feared of waking him before they were done with their treachery and betrayal. *Maybe they hadn't had to fear, because of the drug Valarda had slipped into the wine she served him the night before.*

For, from the vile, oily taste on his tongue, and the little hot red throb of pain behind his eyes, Ryker guessed that he had been drugged. He had been drugged once before, while those he thought were friends had robbed him and left him to die, and he remembered the effects of it well.

A thirst for vengeance came into him then, like a cold black poison in his blood.

Those who had betrayed him that time before had left him to die, like this—bound and helpless for the first cliff dragon or sandcat who came near, hunting meat.

But he had fooled them.

He had endured. He had clung tenaciously to life with an iron grip. And he had lived. Lived to hunt them down, those three, one by one, though half a world lay between them.

And he had taken his revenge, slowly, one at a time, enjoying it. Afterwards, he had not liked remembering what he had done, but he did not regret the doing of it. For a man pays his debts, every last debt, or he is something less than a man.

Staring at the empty day with hard, slitted eyes, Ryker knew that he would pay this debt, too. On the boy; on the old man; and—yes—even on the girl. The girl he had been very near to loving. . . .

"If you're done feeling sorry for yourself, *F'yagh,*" said Zarouk quietly, "roll over here beside me. There is a knife slid down my boot, but as my hands are tied I cannot reach it. Maybe you can. If so, cut me free, and I will free your hands, and the priest's."

"You'll slit my throat first, and you know it," grunted Ryker.

Prince Zarouk shrugged. "Why should I bother? We'll all die here—of thirst, or of the fangs of the first beast that comes this way. Unless you cut me free."

"You'll blood your knife in me the moment your hands are free, because you hate my guts."

The prince looked at him. "I have no love for you, scum of the *F'yagha.* But there are those whom I hate more than you. You know the truth of that, because you hate them too—the friends you rescued from the mob back in Yeolarn, who betrayed you here while you slept, and stole away like thieves in the night, leaving you to die. You hate them, too, more than you hate Zarouk, who has done you no particular hurt.''

Ryker said nothing. He could not deny the truth of what Zarouk said, but swallowing it left a bitter taste.

''Come, man, fight for life, don't lie there pitying yourself!'' the prince said levelly. ''I would be a fool to slay you now, even if I could. When the beasts come—as they *will* come, unless my laggardly men get here first— we'll have a better chance at living longer, two strong men to stand against them. The priest is nothing, you know that, half-mad, and old and feeble. I cannot fight the dragons of the cliffs alone, armed only with a slim knife. But the two of us, together, we might live. *To be revenged someday on those who left us here.*''

Ryker sighed, knowing he was a damned fool, and rolled over to where the desert-hawk sat, and began fumbling for the knife thrust down into his boot. He found it after a time, and inched it out. Then, with numb fingers and aching wrists, he sawed clumsily at the thongs that bound Zarouk's hands—sawing at the flesh of those hands, as often as not, although the prince neither winced nor cried out at the pain of it.

After a long while, Zarouk was free. He chafed his wrists until the circulation began to return, then got up and went over to where Dmu Dran lay, and cut his bonds.

Then he strode over to where Ryker lay in a huddle and stood looking down at him, smiling slightly, fingering the knife.

Ryker said nothing. But he gave him look for look, and there was no weakness in his face, no trace of fear.

The prince knelt and cut his hands free. Then he stood

up and put the knife into his sleeve, and went to look over the cliff edge, and searched the desert with narrowed eyes.

As soon as he had rubbed the numbness from his stiff muscles, Ryker came over to where Zarouk stood.

"What now?" he asked.

Zarouk shrugged.

"Now we sit down and wait until my men get here," he said flatly. "After that, we'll see."

Ryker nodded thoughtfully. Then he found a convenient boulder and sat down. And waited.

To learn whether he was going to live or die.

# III
## The Door to Zhiam

## 11. The Lost Nation

AFTER THE MEN had tired of using the whips on him, they left him hanging there in the chains all night without water. He was half unconscious most of the time; the rest of the time he was a little mad, and would have raved if his tongue were not black and swollen from thirst.

With dawn they relented and cut him down, and let the *F'yagh* who was their other captive tend to his cold wounds and lacerated back. Through a blood-dimmed haze Ryker caught glimpses of this man, a white man, an Earthsider, whom he had never seen before and whose name he knew not.

Nor cared. What mattered was that the Earthman gave him *water*. Cool, sweet, blessed water—more wondrous than any wine, more precious than rubies. He drank, and drank, and fell into a doze. And woke to find the man working over him.

He opened the older wounds and cleaned the pus out of them and soothed them with creamy ointments filled with drugs that numbed the pain and drained the poison and held death at bay. Then he shot Ryker full of antibacterials and fever fighters and fed him hot, delicious broth until he fell asleep again. This time it was a wholesome sleep from which, when he woke, he woke refreshed and strengthened and—sane.

Zarouk's men called him the Dok-i-Tar, which was the nearest they could bend their tongues around "doctor." The People have no word in their language for a savant, a scientist, a man who devotes his life to the gathering of knowledge with a selfless fervor that is almost religious. Such a man, Ryker soon learned, was Eli Herzog, an Israeli by nationality, a Martian by exile, a scientist and philosopher by nature.

He was an old man with a tall brow and a big nose and not much hair. What there was of it was thin and white and silky. His eyes were watery, gentle, wise, filled with humor and wistful dreams, but without illusions.

They were exactly the eyes of another Jewish savant, a man named Einstein, in the famous portrait by Roether which Ryker had seen once, years ago, in the great museum on Luna.

Like that other great mind, Herzog loved humanity as he loved knowledge, but he had no delusions about the sanctity of either. He had been exiled to Mars twenty years before, for so-called political "crimes" back on Earth— during "The Troubles" merely to express an opinion that differed from the official line was defined as criminal.

On Earth, then, Doc Herzog had been a criminal. Here, he was more like a saint. He fell in love with the People and with their ancient ways and traditions. He loved them for their pride and their poverty, their grimly cherished honor, and their refusal to yield one inch before the overwhelming might of Earth and all her millions and her machines.

He had devoted all the remainder of his life to the study of their civilization. Science had changed much by this century. Back in the 1900s, an astrophysicist was an astrophysicist, an archaeologist was an archaeologist, and seldom the twain did meet. Today, things were different, and Herzog knew as much about both topics as he knew about Martian literature and myth, or comparative anthropology, or nine-dimensional geometric theory, or null-state mathematics—which was plenty. He was a Synthesist, with a dozen or thirteen doctorates in as many different fields. Since he was a doctor thirteen times over, Ryker decided to call him simply "Doc," and they left it at that.

Zarouk had picked him up several months ago down in Chryse, hunting for petroglyphs. Since Dok-i-Tars of his sort have great powers of healing, and Zarouk had a lieutenant who had been badly mauled by a sandcat, his men captured the old *F'yagh*. Herzog had an M.D. tucked away among those thirteen doctorates, so it was no great feat for him to bring the man back to health. But Zarouk thought it was a marvel, and kept the old Dok-i-Tar around as a sort of good-luck talisman.

Doc Herzog didn't care. All of this planet was one vast laboratory to his way of thinking, and it didn't matter very much which part of it he was in.

Indeed, as a member of Zarouk's retinue, he had been introduced to many discoveries he might otherwise never have found.

"Such as?" grunted Ryker, wincing as the doctor massaged the stiffness from his scarred shoulders.

"Why, this very city, my boy! Always a myth I have thought it. And here I am, big as life! You don't know where you are, do you?"

"Beats me," said Ryker. "Just one of the Dead Cities, that's all I know."

"Oh, more than that, my boy—much more! The inscriptions have never been defaced, I, even, can read them." His eyes grew wistful, dreaming, and his dry croak of a voice softened to a reverent, hushed whisper. "Khuu, the Last Encampment. Here is the place the Lost

95

Nation fled to, after wars; here was it they rested for a century, more, maybe, before going on to the end of their road.''

A cold tingle traveled the length of Ryker's spine. Hardened though he was, he felt his hackles lift. This was a place whispered about in the myths of Mars, and those myths were older than the very mountains of the Earth.

''Khuu!'' he repeated. ''Cripes, Doc—I always thought that was just one of their legends, like, you know —like Lost Illinios, and Yhoom, and the Valley Where Life Began, and all the rest of it!* D'you mean it's really true, and we're really here?''

''Oh, it's true enough, and here we are,'' Doc said softly. ''Here, where the Lost Nation camped awhile, before vanishing from the knowledge of men forever. Now drink this, and shut up for a bit.''

Ryker downed the fluid, and napped for a while, as his wounds healed and his body mended. But he had plenty to chew on. He had lived and moved among the People long enough to have heard of the Lost Nation, and it troubled him—but why, he could not have said.

Once, long ago, at the beginnings of history, there had been ten nations sharing this planet between them. Apart, yet together; different, yet the same; and united in their worship of the Timeless Ones, and in their loyalty to the Jammad Tengru, as the holy emperor was called.

Then one nation had fallen from the ancient ways,

---

*For more about this valley, the Martian equivalent of the Garden of Eden, see my recent novel *The Valley Where Time Stood Still* (1974), available in hardcovers from Doubleday, and in paperback from Popular Library.

turned aside to worship a new god, forgetting the old faith and severing the old alliance. The Jammad Tengru who had ruled all of Mars in that distant age had declared them anathema—had, in effect, excommunicated them. And nine nations rode to war, to holy war, to *jehad,* against the rebels.

Broken by the war, but not defeated, the tenth nation had fled into the north, paused to lick their wounds in the northernmost of the old cities, and then—

History was silent on their doom. Even the myths hinted little. And to this day, no man could say what had become of the outlaw nation. Even its name and totem were forgotten in the mists of the remote past.

All memory of this event had been erased from monuments and chronicles. The People themselves had tried to forget that it had ever happened. But mysteries die hard, and live long on the lips of men.

And this was the story of the Lost Nation.

And now Ryker thought he knew the secret of the riddle, and the solution of the oldest mystery known to man.

*Zhaggua!*

The word meant "devil."

Might it not also mean "devil-worshipper"?

Far into the north the Lost Nation had fled in the beginning of time. Somewhere in the hoarfrosted desert-lands near the pole it had vanished from the knowledge of men.

And north was the road Valarda and her accomplices had been taking. Were they living descendants of the Lost Nation? Zarouk, perhaps, did not call them devils for nothing. Why had they come down out of their hidden realm? For the black stone seal he had taken from an ancient tomb? And why had they gone back into the north, having thieved it from him?

*Were they . . . going home?*

Nothing could live in the frigid realms around the pole, Ryker knew. In ancient days, perhaps it had been warm and fertile, as once the polar regions of Earth had been, as scientists had known for centuries from oil deposits found in northern Greenland and the fossilized remains of prehistoric forests unearthed in Canada.

Once, aeons ago, perhaps the Martian Arctic had been ice and snow, too—frozen water. But no longer was this true. It had not been true for endless ages.

The ice-fields around the pole are composed of frozen carbon dioxide—"dry ice"—and nothing that lives and breathes could dwell in that bleak, dry, burning hell of incredible cold.

*Unless it lived—underground.*

There were vast caverns beneath the crust of Mars, Ryker knew, and labyrinthine systems of subterranean tunnels, extending for hundreds of miles. There dwelt the giant albino rodents, called *orthave,* which the People hunt for furs.

At least, this was true of the Southlands with which Ryker was more familiar. But might it not be true as well, here in the north?

Who could say?

Ryker had a grim hunch that before long he would be finding out.

If they let him live long enough, that is.

The next day the raiders broke camp and began the long trek north. Houm's caravan went with them. By now Ryker had put two and two together, coming up with four.

Houm was an agent of Zarouk, as Goro the Juhagir was. Houm's trading expedition was a fake. The wains contained food supplies and weapons, nothing more. Houm had lurked here and there in the country north of Yeolarn, awaiting word that the devil worshippers had either been taken or had eluded capture.

If they escaped, they would be heading north. And Yhakhah was the jumping-off-point for the north. So, when apprised of Valarda's escape, Houm had ridden hard for the oasis town, to be there ready and waiting. The trap had functioned perfectly.

And Goro was Zarouk's spy. Probably he had been in Yeolarn when Valarda danced and the mob tried to stone her. Very likely, Goro had taken no part in that mob, but had merely watched and waited from a place of safety and concealment. And when it became obvious that the three *zhaggua* and their Earthling dupe had fled the city, he had somehow conveyed word of this both to Zarouk in the south, and Houm in the north. Then he had made rendezvous with the prince his master, and together they had ridden hard for the Lost City, where, according to a prearranged plan, Houm and his fake caravan were loitering.

Goro was needed, for only he had actually seen the three devil worshippers, and only he could identify them for certain. Once he and Zarouk had seen Valarda dance, the search was over. And that very night, just before dawn, the trap had closed, and the hawks had seized their prey.

It would have gone beautifully, save for the maverick behavior of Ryker. But in the end, all things even out. And now, even though Valarda and Melandron and Kiki had escaped, it was known where they were headed.

*North.*

Beyond the dust desert of Meroe.

Across the narrow isthmus that connects the twin continental land masses of Casius and Boreosyrtis.

And into the shadow haunted, the trackless, the unmapped, the mysterious boreal desert called Umbra.

*Umbra—the Shadowed Land.*

They had named it uncannily well, had the old Earthling astronomers and mapmakers. For that dim arctic realm has been under the shadow of an ancient curse and an age-old mystery since Mars was young and warm and burgeoning with life.

Into the Umbra the Lost Nation had ridden, long ago.

Somewhere in the Umbra they had vanished from human ken, in the morning of time.

*And there, in that bleak arctic waste, pockmarked with ancient craters, where the dry dust drifted under a cold, whispering wind, rose the timeless enigma of the Pteraton, the Sphinx of Mars.*

Did it mark the entrance to an underground world?

## 12. The Keystone

THEY CROSSED THE desert, retracing the flight of Ryker and the others, and ascended to the top of the plateau, their beasts scrambling awkwardly up the steps of the eroded rock strata.

That night they camped on top of the narrow isthmus that once, perhaps, had linked two small continents, and against whose ancient and crumbling ramparts the long vanished oceans of Mars had once broken in flying foam.

Ryker wasn't sure why they had let him live, or why they bothered to bring him along, but he didn't much care. Revenge filled his heart like cold, heavy lead, and at least when Zarouk caught up with the three devil worshippers, Ryker would be in at the kill.

He shared wine that night with Zarouk, and fat Houm, and the little priest. Oddly, the desert prince seemed no longer to bear him any ill will. The red, terrible ordeal at the whipping post, perhaps, had satisfied Zarouk's hunger for revenge against the *F'yagh* who had spoiled his fun, captured and humiliated him.

For the moment, anyway, he seemed satisfied. But Ryker wasn't so sure. Men like Zarouk seldom forget a grudge. There would be a final reckoning later on, he thought. Right now, probably Zarouk kept him alive because he thought he might have a use for him.

When Xinga, the chief of the caravan guards, whom Ryker now understood to be one of Zarouk's chieftains, came to fetch him to the tent of the prince for wine, Ryker went without a word. He could not be more completely in Zarouk's power than he was already, so what the hell.

The wine was cold and sour and strong, and Ryker savored it, listening to the conversation.

Zarouk asked what he knew of Valarda's ultimate destination, and Ryker told him—truthfully enough—that he knew nothing at all. Oddly, Zarouk seemed to believe him. So Ryker tried a question of his own, testing this new spirit of acceptance.

"Was it your men who hunted me out of the New City, and herded me into Yeolarn?" he asked. And he was surprised at the reply.

Zarouk burst out laughing, a harsh bark of laughter, true enough, but there was genuine humor in it.

"Poor dupe, it was the boy all the time—didn't you know?" he grinned.

Ryker blinked.

"The boy? *What* boy?"

"Valarda's imp, what's his name—"

"Kiki, d'you mean?"

The desert prince nodded.

"Didn't you even guess that? The little devil—why do you think the woman brought him along?"

Ryker didn't know, and said as much.

Dmu Dran spoke now, his voice a thin whisper.

"The creature is a *quaraph*," he said. And the nape-hairs at the back of Ryker's neck stirred as to a chill wind.

*A quaraph!* Ryker shook himself numbly: the naked imp was a telepath—a Sensitive! The telepathic gene was more common among Martians than Earthsiders, he had heard, but still rare enough.

And now he began to understand how they had played him like a fish on a hook.

*No one* had hunted him out of the New City and through

the winding ways of old Yeolarn. They had merely made him believe that it was so. Or Kiki had, anyway.

For a person who can read the thoughts passing through your mind finds it easy enough to *insert* thoughts into that mind. A telepath gifted and skillful enough can even convince your senses that they see or hear or taste or even smell things that are not really there.

They had played him for a sucker, all right.

He drank the wine moodily.

"Why me?" he asked at last.

The hunched little priest spoke up again.

"The stone seal you found in the old tomb, *F'yagh*," he whispered between thin lips. "We know that it is somehow precious to the accursed *zhaggua*, although we do not know how or why. 'The Keystone,' the old texts name it. Its magic opens the door that leads to their hidden domain. Long ago it was stolen from them, and they want it back."

"How did they know I had the thing?" grunted Ryker.

The priest stared at him with eyes as cold as a serpent's.

"Long ago there was one among the *zhaggua* who rebelled from their evil ways, and who thieved the Keystone from its secret place. By it he came again into this world of ours, he and his followers. But we of the *hualatha,* we priests of the Timeless Ones, knew him for what he truly was from his eyes of evil golden flame, and slew him and all who followed him. We buried that one in unhallowed ground, together with all that he had carried with him out of Black Zhiam. My brothers of the *hualatha* in that long-ago time knew naught of the nature of the Keystone, and buried him with it, you see."

"No, I don't see," the Earthling said. "But keep talking."

"The Door to Zhiam was thus left open, and could not

be sealed again unless it was done with the Keystone. The *zhaggua*, the devil worshippers, they knew it was in the outside world, but not where, for although there exists a strange affinity between their *quaraphs* and the substance whereof the Keystone is wrought, the holy signs cut like sigils upon the doors of that man's tomb kept them from detecting the place where it was hidden.''

Ryker nodded slowly: it was all beginning to make sense, at last.

"Go on," he said.

But Zarouk took up the tale.

Toying absently with his winecup, he said, "The moment you broke into the tomb and thus destroyed the magic of the priests, the Sensitives among the devil-men in Black Zhiam knew of it. In time their emissaries ventured out into the world of men once again, to search for you, and to rob you of the stone. They could come and go freely from Zhiam, as Dmu Dran has said, because the way was left open."

"And until the stone was theirs, and they could close the door again," said fat Houm softly, "they would not be safe from the vengeance of men, no, not even in far Zhiam."

"What is this Zhiam?" Ryker inquired.

The priest, the prince and the merchant exchanged a glance, then shrugged.

"No reason why you should not know," said Zarouk. "It is the name of their land. We neither know where it is, nor how it has been kept hidden all this while. But we shall find it."

Ryker studied him curiously.

"Listen, Zarouk, there's something about all this that doesn't quite fit," he said.

"Ask, then," shrugged the desert prince.

"You don't strike me as particularly devout," said Ryker. "Why are you so interested in all of this? What's in it for you? There's got to be something more than meets the eye in all this, something beyond just religion."

Zarouk grinned, then threw back his head and laughed. He slapped Ryker's shoulder, shaking his head.

"Earthling, may the Timeless Ones forgive me, but I like you—*F'yagh* or no *F'yagh*! We are alike, you and I, though we were born on different worlds. Of course, you know there is more here than just holy matters. Tell him, Houm."

The merchant fingered his small beard, eyes clever and sly.

"Treasure, Ryker. And more than gold, much more: *power.* Power enough to break the hold of the accursed *F'yagha* on this world, and drive them hence. Power enough to topple the Nine Princes, and weld their hordes into one empire, under one throne—with a warlord to lead them such as this planet has not seen in thrice ten thousand years!"

Ryker grinned without humor. This was talk he could understand. These were motives he knew and believed in.

"And on that throne . . . Zarouk the Hawk?" he guessed.

The eyes of the desert prince flashed proud fires. Then he smiled cunningly, yet approvingly.

"I told you that this man was for us," he said purringly. "I sensed it in my blood. In my bones! Yes, Ryker, *power.* Power enough to take this world apart, and put it back together again—for *us.* Houm is in it for the wealth, being Houm; and Dmu Dran is in it for the extermination of an ancient heresy, being what he is. *And I mean to rule this world, someday* . . . then, ah, then! Those who scorned me, and derided me, and named me outlaw and

105

renegade, and cast me out, and hunted me, and made war upon me: well, there will come a reckoning, Ryker. And it will be sweet, that reckoning!''

His purring voice was sleek as silk. But the rasp of steel was in the sound of it, and Ryker grinned a little, showing his teeth. It would not be comfortable to be Zarouk's enemy, when the day of his power dawned.

''The power of their magic, aye, accursed and devil-bought though it may be,'' the prince continued softly. ''Once, with strange weapons of power, they broke the nations, though it was nine against one. They would have conquered, too, but something went wrong. We know not what, but they retreated into the north, into Zhiam. They still possess those weapons. And with them the Hawk of the Desert shall not spare the Nine Nations, as once the devil-people of Zhiam spared them! Oh, no! With that unholy magic I shall shatter the world to bits, and mold my empire from the fragments. And *you*, Ryker, there is a place in all of this for you. You can share in the glory of my triumph. Wealth, Ryker, and women! Everything you want, everything that you have ever desired. I will give it all to you, and a place near the throne, as well.''

''I thought we'd be getting around to me sooner or later,'' Ryker grunted. ''I knew you hadn't kept me alive just because you like my face. Well, let's get down to it. What use do you have for me?''

''The stone, Ryker, the black seal. The Keystone. They will have used it to lock the Door to Zhiam behind them. We need you for that.''

Ryker stared at the hawk-faced prince.

''But . . . I don't have it!'' he burst out. ''They took it from me, there when we camped that night, when they took my guns!''

''I know,'' smiled Zarouk. ''But the secret of the Keystone lies within your brain, Ryker. The mind never forgets, the priests tell us. Everything the eyes have seen, are preserved in the memories of the mind—flawless, perfect, to the last detail.''

"The stone whereof the Key was fashioned is the same black crystal stuff whereof the *zhaggua* made Pteraton," said Houm. "We believe the power of the Keystone resides in the substance of that stone, and in the exact proportions of the design and the inscription.''

"And we mean to have it from you, *F'yagh*," said the gaunt priest. "Willingly, we hope, for that will make it easier. But willingly or not, we mean to have it. If we have to tear it from your mind with hot red pain, *F'yagh*—"

"But, surely, it will not come to that," said Zarouk, soothingly. "Ryker is a man of sense: a man like unto us, my brothers! He wants from life the good things gold can buy, is it not so? And there will be much gold, Ryker, when the very world is ours . . . gold enough to drown a man in, Ryker . . . and women, Ryker, women like tawny cats . . . women as smooth as silk, as warm as satin. . . .''

Despite himself, the throb of desire stirred Ryker's pulse, but he was thinking of only one woman. And Zarouk smiled, guessing the direction of his thoughts.

"Aye, Ryker, you can even have Valarda if you want her," he smiled. "After I am done with her, of course.''

## 13. Into the Shadowed Land

WITH DAWN THE next day, Zarouk's outlaws broke camp and continued across the isthmus to its northern edge. Here they were only a league or less from the maximum southernmost edge of the polar cap, and the cliff wall on this side of the plateau was deeply eroded by the extremes of heat and cold.

They descended the cliffs, and entered into the desert-land of Umbra.

In truth, this was the Shadowed Land. The dim, cool sun of Mars lay very low on the southern horizon, and the cliffs of the ancient plateau cast long shadows into the north, bathing the parched dust of the desert in purple gloom and filling the innumerable impact craters, large and small, with lakes of shadow.

Nowhere did they discern the slightest signs of life. Even the reptiles that make the Southlands dangerous could not exist here, within only a few degrees of the pole. Nor could the hardy lichens, the rubbery pod-vines, the weird blue vegetation of Mars that, by comparison, grew thick and lush in the southern latitudes, cling to life in this empty and desolate dry hell of burning cold.

How, then, could the devil worshippers of the Lost Nation live here? Even in the deepest crater, valley or ravine, the dry burning chill penetrated. It was a mystery.

But, then, the land of legend they called Zhiam had always been that—a mystery.

• • •

Ryker had been left alone to think things over. They let him ride alone, with desert hawks behind him, but his hands were not bound. It was safe enough: in this dry hell, there was no place to go.

He wanted revenge on Valarda for her treachery, her betrayal, yes. As for her people, he cared nothing. Why, after all, should he? For him it had always been a matter of taking care of himself first of all. It was simply a question of survival.

Besides, what did he owe to this unknown people he had never met, never seen? Let them fend for themselves, defend themselves, it was nothing to him what became of them.

The only members of their race he had ever known had lied to him, tricked him, robbed him, and left him bound and helpless, to die. *Let* Zarouk's hawks swoop down upon them, to rend and slash and tear, to burn and rape and pillage! It was nothing to him.

Why, then, did he feel uneasy—obscurely troubled— unsatisfied at heart?

Well, for one thing, he knew he could not trust Zarouk to keep his bargain. Even if Ryker helped him recreate the lost Keystone, there would be no gold or women for Ryker, once Zarouk had from him the service he wanted. There would be a swift knife in the back, and a lonely grave under the shadowy skies.

But in the whirl of battle, the turmoil and confusion of the attack which Zarouk had planned against Black Zhiam, might there not be opportunities aplenty for Ryker to elude his watchers, and get away?

He hoped so. Because it was probably his only chance at living a while longer.

• • •

That night he agreed to cooperate with Zarouk in re-creating the lost Keystone.

It was the hunched, gaunt priest, the fanatical Dmu Dran, who unlocked his memories, while Houm and Zarouk and burly Xinga watched with fascination.

A drug called *phynol* was used. This Zarouk's raiders had thieved from a CA interrogation team. It was a deriva-tive of nitrobarb, chemically allied to sodium pentothal, but very much more effective. All Ryker knew was that he became sleepier and sleepier, finally sinking into a trance state in which his volition was suspended and his uncon-scious rose to the fore. His conscious mind watched on while, at Dmu Dran's bidding, Ryker's hands took up a chunk of black crystal and began to carve.

It was an uncanny experience for Ryker, watching himself perform acts uncontrolled by his conscious will. It was weird, but it was not frightening. The drug induced in him a dreamy, languid euphoria in which no strong emo-tion was possible.

His hands worked machinelike for hours over the piece of hard crystal, shaping it to the precise dimensions his mind remembered with such photographic clarity. And all the while his mind looked on bemused, drifting in a rosy haze of dreams, uncaring.

A second and, later, a third injection of the drug were required. Ryker neither knew nor cared what they were doing to him. In the gentle euphoria of the drug he floated into improbably gorgeous dreams. These, then, were the *phynol* dreams he had heard of. Men became easily ad-dicted to the stuff, he dimly knew, but he cared not at all, drifting through a fairyland of his own creation.

After five hours, the replica was completed. Ryker's body had toiled without rest like a robot, and, if he had not been insulated from reality by the *phynol*, he would have been fearfully aware that the muscles of his hands and wrists and arms were aching with an agonized exhaustion.

But he knew nothing, floating through sunset clouds.

"Sleep, now, *F'yagh*," crooned Dmu Dran.

Obediently, Ryker's mind submerged in waves of darkness which lapped up about him, soothing his weary hands. Every muscle relaxed utterly. He would sleep for hours now, and awaken weary and stiff, but unharmed.

"We could kill him now, lord," suggested Houm. "He is a burden to us, and so long as he is alive, a danger to our plans."

"We could indeed, fat one," murmured the desert prince negligently. "What think you, priest?"

Dmu Dran sat hunched on a stool, cradling the precious oval talisman in his lap, fondling it with trembling hands like fleshless claws. He lifted dull eyes to his master at this query.

"Kill him for what purpose, lord?" whispered the priest in a dry croaking voice, for he too was weary, and for all the hours that the mindless hands of Ryker had toiled over the stone, Dmu Dran had not for one instant relaxed his vigilance.

"He affords no threat to us," the priest said. "Surely, you have warriors enough to watch over him. And we may have need for the Accursed One later."

"What need is that?" asked Houm. "We have the stone. We have everything we require, with it."

Dmu Dran looked at him sleepily.

"And what if the stone does not work, when we employ it?" he asked tonelessly. "What if the hands of Ryker slipped—or wearied—or cut a shade too deep, or too shallow? If we slay the creature now, we cannot use his mind again, should we need it. Better to keep him alive for the time, until the door is unlocked and Zhiam lies open before us."

Zarouk stood up. "I think the priest is right," he said curtly. "We may have to search the mind of Ryker again, and deeper than before. Perhaps the stone does not quite fit, and is not shaped quite properly. Then we can search his memories again—and many times, if needful. Let him live. Xinga, return this offal to its place."

The burly lieutenant touched his palm to the smooth flesh above his heart. Then, stooping, he picked up the unconscious Earthling and tossed him over one broad shoulder like a sack of meal and bore him from the tent.

It was daylight when Ryker awoke. He lay on the floor of one of the wains, which creaked along over the desert dunes. The old savant was there beside him, his fine brow furrowed with care, his gentle eyes worried.

"So, how are you feeling?"

"Like death warmed over, Doc," grunted Ryker, trying to sit up. His tongue felt like burnt leather, and tasted like it, too. His brain was dull, his thoughts sluggish, and he had a headache of champion proportions. But that was as nothing compared to the stiff lameness of his hands and arms. He flexed his fingers, wincing.

"A little massage, maybe," the old man suggested. He began to rub the stiffness from Ryker's aching arms, kneading the weary muscles with surprisingly strong fingers. Later, he gave the big man some powder in a drink of wine that relaxed him and soothed his headache.

After a time, Ryker dozed off. He had not been entirely certain he would ever awaken after cutting the replica of the Keystone for the conspirators. Since they *had* let him live afterwards, he assumed they still had some use for him. So he slept easy, without fears.

When he awoke again it was midday according to the chrono on his wrist. But not like any Martian noon he had ever witnessed before, the dim, weak sun riding low on the horizon to the south, the zenith of heaven black as midnight. They were a lot closer to the pole, he knew, and the wind was cold and dry with an edge that bit into his bones like the blade of a razor.

He shuddered, pulling his cloak of *orthava* furs about him more closely.

Herzog was huddled over his notebook, scribbling, scribbling, and peering nearsightedly at the page.

"Where are we, do you know, Doc?" he muttered.

The old man looked up, and grinned. He had a beautiful smile, despite his ugly face. It was the gentle, open, wondering smile of a little child, naive and vulnerable.

"Awake again, is it? Feeling better now, I hope?"

"Yeah. Where are we?"

"Smack in the middle of the Umbra, my boy. Exactly on the line—north latitude fifty-five degrees, one minute, if I read the stars right, and I think I do. Those hills up ahead to the north are Copais Palus, the border of Cecropia. I never in all my days have been this close to the pole, how about you?"

Ryker shook his head, and it turned into a shiver that shook him from head to foot.

"Me, neither," he growled. "And any closer than this, I got a feeling I don't want to get. Say, is there anything to eat?"


They soon made camp for the night, the drovers maneuvering the beasts, drawing the wagons into a huge half circle. There was no particular reason for this, since no dangerous predators were believed to be able to survive this far into the frostlands. But Houm did not believe in taking unnecessary chances, and since this was the way caravans were always arranged in formation for the night, save in a town, he saw no reason to change the customary way of doing things.

Besides, it was not entirely impossible that the Lost Nation had scouts or sentries watching the outskirts of Zhiam. Surely, if Valarda and her accomplices had reached Zhiam by now, as they undoubtedly had, the devil warriors would be warned of the possible approach of enemies. A night attack was far from impossible. So Zarouk bade Xinga post guards about the perimeter and commanded that they should be on the alert for anything.

They ate that night under the weird banner of the aurora. Flickering, wavering banners of ghostly fire glowed against the gloom of the north. The desert men mumbled half-forgotten prayers, signing themselves with holy signs that were supposed to keep the devils away, and that night each man had a pan of green fire near him as he slept.

Doc Herzog, however, was enthralled. He had known that Mars was presumed to have its own equivalent of Earth's famous "northern lights," but had never before seen them for himself, having only heard the tales the travelers told. Long after Ryker turned in, the old savant still sat up, staring at the sky and making notes.

# 14. The Sphinx of Mars

THE NEXT DAY they came at last within sight of their goal. It was clearly visible a long way off, like a mountain. But this was no mountain. Perhaps, once, long ago, it had been an immense outcropping of pure mineral, thrust up from the bowels of the planet by the action of geological forces. Or—again, just possibly—it had been an enormous meteorite, or a small asteroid, drawn down to the surface of Mars by gravitational forces.

Whatever it once had been, it was now like nothing that any of them had ever seen.

The explorers and scientists who had come here after Christoffsen had seen it first from the air. Foil-winged skimmers, as the flimsy aircraft are called, are the only craft that can sustain themselves aloft in the thin atmosphere of Mars. With them, Exploration Teams One through Seven had circumnavigated Mars, photomapping the terrain with continuously operating cameras. Later, specialists had constructed a mosaic from these band segments. Then it had been discovered.

*The Sphinx of Mars*, the stereovision newscasters had named it back Earthside. No other name was conceivable for the stone enigma. Like that other Sphinx—aeons younger, and not very much larger, and only a little less mysterious—the Sphinx of Mars, too, crouches amidst the waste, hewn anciently into the likeness of a gigantic beast.

But, where the Sphinx of Egypt resembles a human-headed lion, its elder sister near the north pole of Mars is shaped like a crouching insect-thing.

The Pteraton (as it is most accurately named) is a creature from the mythology of the Martians, and could never have been copied from life. The twelve-legged insect, with its four, folded dragonfly wings, fanged mandibles, pear-shaped casque of a head, and three domed compound eyes, is an impossible beast drawn from fancy. Flying insects, in any case, never existed on Mars, as the fossil record demonstrates, and no true insect ever had twelve legs and triplex eyes.

No, the stone enigma of the Pteraton is a beast of fable, even as the woman-headed Sphinx has its origins in fable. Outside of body lice, and the foot-long roachlike subterranean scavengers called *xunga*, who infest certain of the Southland caverns, insects are unknown on Mars. So any vague, distorted resemblance the stone monster bears to a cross between ant, dragonfly, spider and grasshopper— improbably and monstrously rolled into one—is a testimony to the inventive imagination of the mythographers of prehistoric Mars.

The thing cast an eerie pall upon their spirits, however.

The stone whereof it had been carved was a black crystalloid like jet, also in a way like quartz, and hard as basalt. It glittered weirdly in the dying light, and the geometrical facets of its three hemispheric eyes caught and held the sun-dazzle. It seemed to stare at them with fathomless eyes, its ugly, bony jaws fixed in a grin of menace.

It was uncanny. Ryker had seen depth photos of the Pteraton many times. But the reality was awesome, even intimidating, while the pictures had only been quaint and curious.

The beasts did not like it here, he noticed.

Generally, *slidars* are either restive and quarrelsome, or phlegmatic and stolid. Now, in the presence of that mountainous sculptured monster that loomed up before them like some black, alien god from the depths of time, they shied, clawed at the ground, uttering that ear-piercing squeal that is the loper's equivalent of a stallion's nervous whinny.

"Here we make camp," said Zarouk, swinging down from the saddle.

Their food supplies were running low, for the desert trip had been somewhat lengthier than they had presumed it might be. While some of the men put up tents and others drew the wains into position, Xinga dispatched certain of his warriors into the waste to scavenge.

Martian warriors live off the land, and a first-class scrounger is a prized member of any war party. Even a pack of desert marauders like Zarouk's band could not carry sufficient stores with them on their forays, and were forced to hunt for food.

But there was no food to be had here in the Umbra, where nothing lived or could live.

"We'd best be to it, then, and swiftly," muttered Raith, glancing nervously over his shoulder at the crouching stone beast. The whites of his eyes showed, and he licked bearded lips uneasily. Raith was as superstitious as any other ignorant barbarian, but braver and tougher than many. Even he, Ryker noticed, kept glancing quickly at the mountainous black crystal, as if at any moment he expected it to . . . *move.*

"Yeah," Ryker nodded. "If we don't get to Zhiam soon, we'll starve here. Unless we run out of wine or water first, that is."

The warrior swore under his breath, and tugged the

thongs. Together, without speaking further, they raised the tent on its collapsable poles. Then Raith strode off, shoulders hunched against the cold, unwinking gaze of the crouching monster.

Ryker looked after him, thoughtfully. He knew Raith better than any of the other desert men, for a bond of unacknowledged comradeship had grown between them from the moment he had ended the hazing by knocking Raith down.

Like many another strong man, Raith admired a man stronger than he. Neither said anything much about it, but they were as close to being friends as a *F'yagh* and a warrior of the People can become.

And Ryker knew Raith well, liked him, trusted him in certain ways, and respected him more than a little. He was a good man, and better than most in Zarouk's band.

And if Raith—even Raith—was this jumpy, this edgy, so early on, then Zarouk was going to be in trouble before long, Ryker realized. At the thought he showed his white teeth in a hard grin that had little humor in it.

Zarouk had to find Zhiam soon. If he didn't pull off a miracle, his own men would mutiny on him.

The notion pleased Ryker. He chuckled over it all the way back to where his steed crouched restive and nervous, waiting to be unsaddled.

Zarouk and his men circled the stone monument, looking for an entrance of some sort. With spear butts they tested the sides of the statue, listening for the echo that would reveal that here, at least, the monument was hollow.

Cracks or pits in the surface, where regular or aligned, they tried to pry open with the points of their knife blades, searching for a secret door.

Here and there, at intervals around the circuit of the

118

stone monster, they dug pits, thinking that the entrance might be buried in the dust.

They found nothing at all.

Under the fires of sunset, and, later, under the incredibly lavish brilliance of the stars, and the uncanny witch-fires of the quivering aurora, they searched on.

Ryker and the scientist watched them for a while.

He had shared with Doc his idea that Zhiam might be situated in an enormous cavern under the Sphinx. Herzog did not seem to take his theory with any particular seriousness.

"Why under the Sphinx, of all places?"

"I dunno," Ryker muttered. "'Cause that's where Zarouk's been heading, all this while. Seems he thinks the monument marks the entrance to Zhiam. Well, there's nothing around here for kilometers, except rock and dust. So it *must* be underground, if there's any such place as Zhiam."

Doc mused, tilting his head on one side, looking down at the ground. He kicked against a rock absently, then knelt and fingered a handful of soil. Then, shaking his head, he got to his feet again, dusting off his hands.

"Sandstone," he muttered to himself. "Shale. Not going to be finding any caves in this stuff, my boy! Down south, why, sure. Igneous rock, volcanic origin. Pocket of gas trapped when the liquid stuff began to cool—"

"Yeah? What about erosion—underground rivers—that sort of thing," argued Ryker.

"Don't know any underground rivers on Mars," said Herzog positively. "Erosion, is it? The kind of stuff this ground has under it, you could erode forever, my boy, and any cavern you made would just crumble and fall in. Forget about underground caverns! If Zhiam is supposed to be here, and isn't here, then it's—somewhere else."

119

"But where?"

Doc would voice no opinion on that.

From his circumambulatory expedition, Zarouk came back looking wrathful. He strode into his tent without speaking, leaving Dmu Dran, who had accompanied him, standing outside. The men who had dug and probed and tapped went to their squads, looking tired and disgruntled.

Grumblings were heard from the men. They little liked camping in this ominous spot, under the shadow of the gigantic crouching stone monster. And they didn't like Zarouk's failure to find the Door.

There was going to be trouble.

At meat, Zarouk was in a vile temper, snapping at Dmu Dran, insulting Houm, and thrashing one of his servants who spilled half a cup of wine.

The scroungers had come limping back into camp, weary and surly and bad tempered. They had found nothing—neither water nor food of any kind. Luckily, it was the six-month-long summer of Mars, or carbon dioxide hoarfrost would have been ankle deep everywhere, fraying tempers even more, and making any trip more painful and difficult.

With no chance of replenishing their larder, the raiders were forced to sharply cut back on their meals to prolong the life of their supplies. Strong men get hungry after hard days of riding, and they get thirsty, too. They aren't happy when the meals get meager and the drink gets scarce.

Tempers flared, and quarreling was common.

Zarouk would have to have some good luck, soon. *Very* soon. That miracle he was going to have to come up with was needed badly already. Time was running out.

He surprised them all—and himself, as well—by producing it the very next day.

They had been probing and poking and tapping away at the insect idol again, for dreary hours. Then, suddenly, a wild, savage yell rang out. Men froze where they were, their blood running cold, mouths suddenly dry.

Then they started to gather from all over the camp. Ryker came thumping up, to find men transfixed with amazement and delight around the front of the Sphinx.

Four of its twelve multiple-jointed limbs were folded before it, like the outstretched paws of the Egyptian Sphinx.

The frontal curve of its thorax was a sheer, smooth surface of black crystal.

*Now, in that wall of glistening jet, a doorway yawned.*

## 15. Black Labyrinth

RYKER NEVER FOUND out which of the desert men it was who had found the secret catch—a simple thing, a loose square of stone which, when pressed, swung counterweights within the thorax of the Sphinx, causing a massive slab of black crystal to sink into the ground. Nor did it really matter.

What mattered was that the way was open. And, wherever and whatever Zhiam truly was, this must be the entrance to that lost realm of legend. For what other reason would the entrance into the hollow monument have been so carefully concealed, unless it led down to Zhiam?

Zarouk was exultant, and fat Houm ebullient. The desert hawk barked orders. Men scurried to arm themselves, while Dmu Dran scuttled away to procure the precious Keystone replica from its place of safety.

This was, quite obviously, the first of at least two such doors. And the second door, it seemed, was locked in such a manner that only the stone seal could open it. Although how you employ a palm-sized scarab-shaped piece of stone in lieu of a key remained to be seen.

The prince wasn't worrying about that, obviously. It was sufficient to take one thing at a time.

Doc Herzog was ecstatic. Only a handful of scholars or scientists had studied the Pteraton as yet, the Colonial Administration's budget for archaeological research being skimpy at best. They had taken extensive depth photos, measured the monument, secured samples of the black crystalling rock from which it had been carved, and that was about the extent of their research thus far. The possibility that the huge idol was hollow and contained chambers or passages, perhaps filled with records or inscriptions, was a tantalizing theory.

But—until now—only that: a theory. Now he was an eye-witness to the discovery of the proof of that theory.

Within an hour and a half, Zarouk's force was ready to enter the capacious interior of the stone enigma.

About twenty-five warriors and drovers were commanded to remain outside. It was their task to guard and keep open Zarouk's escape route, should retreat be necessary. They would guard the camp, tend to the beasts, and protect the wagons and other gear.

One hundred and fifty warriors, heavily armed, followed their Prince through the secret portal into the interior of the Sphinx. With them went Ryker and the old Israeli scientist. The advance guard was led by Xinga, with Zarouk commanding the main body. Raith was left behind in charge of the camp guard, with Goro to keep an eye on him.

Ryker wondered if he would ever see him again.

They filed through the portal into complete darkness. Torches of woven plant fibre, soaked in the fire chemical, lit their way. Ryker found himself in a narrow, low-roofed corridor, walled and floored with slabs of black crystal.

The air here was musty and stale. Obviously, the monument was virtually air tight, and had been sealed for a very long period. The men gasped for breath, and the chemical torches burn feebly.

The corridor ran for a length, turned at right angles to itself, then doubled back.

The silence was stifling. Thousands of tons of solid

rock drank in every sound, muffling even the echoes of boot leather scraping across the dusty floor as men walked carefully, testing every foot of the way before them, alert for concealed deadfalls or mantraps.

The curious acoustical effect fascinated the old savant, but everybody else found it uncomfortable. In the ghastly green light of the torches, men's features looked weirdly distorted, all rolling eyeballs, open mouths, cheeks greasy with sweat. They resembled a legion of the dead, on their way to hell.

After a time, the second corridor ended at the head of a long flight of stone steps, which descended into unknown depths of velvety blackness.

"Look!" the old Israeli said, pointing. "We must be underneath the monument by now, for, see, the steps are cut out of the sandstone of the plain."

Ryker held his torch high, peering into blackness. Doc was right, he saw. A thin, faint breeze blew up from unguessable depths below, smelling sour and dusty. He stifled a sneeze.

The warriors were descending the stone steps now, muttering and clutching each other, fearful of falling. Ryker and Herzog stood backed against the wall, waiting their turn to descend.

Doc rubbed the flat of his hands over the wall, mumbling to himself.

"No inscriptions," he was saying. "That's funny. I think there should be inscriptions. . . ."

Then it was their turn. Holding the old man's arm in case his foot should slip. lifting his torch high before him to light the way, Ryker began to climb down the stairs.

There was no telling how far down into the depths of the planet the sandstone stair might descend. It seemed to go on forever.

And they had no way of guessing what they might find at the bottom, either. But it began to look as if Ryker had had the right idea, after all. Zhiam must be an immense cavern-world, hollowed out beneath the crust of Mars, whether this was geologically impossible, as Doc claimed, or not. What else could it possibly be?

At the bottom of the stairs, space widened out into an enormous square chamber, hewn from the solid rock, and braced and supported by girderlike pillars and arches of metal.

It was a peculiar color, this metal, richly blue-green, as if enameled in an amalgam of jade and malachite. But Ryker had seen its like before. The alloy was unique to Mars, strong and light and unrusting. "Martium," the first explorers had named it, and the metal was widely used for construction, and even exported to Earth as a novelty.

Set into one wall facing the bottom steps of the stone stair, was an immense circular portal of the same gleaming, jewel-toned metal. The shape of this door, if door is what it was, was odd. It was perfectly circular, with the bottom curve of the circle touching, as it were, the stone floor.

There were no hinges, no handles, and no keyhole. The huge metal disk seemed imbedded in the sandstone of the wall, fixed and immobile. But it *must* be a door of some kind, for what else could it be?

Doc cried out, pointing.

Carved in the sandstone above the door in a half circle, was an inscription!

Dmu Dran had been puzzling over it, but seemed unable to make out its meaning, for all his knowledge of the antique lore. Zarouk turned to Herzog, impatiently.

"Can you read that writing, old man?" he demanded. Doc peered at it thoughtfully, his eyes bright, head held a little to one side.

Then, slowly—reverently—he nodded.

"It is in the oldest known form of the Hieratic script," he whispered. "Even older than that, maybe. I can make it out well enough, I guess. But no one in the world speaks this dialect, or has, for millions and millions of years."

"Read it, then! Xinga—hold the torches steady."

The old scientist peered at the inscription, moving his lips silently. Then he spoke aloud.

*"Dja-ih az Mhu-á Zhiam-aZar."*

"Which means?" demanded Zarouk hoarsely.

" 'This is the Door to . . . Outside-the-World,' " said the old man.

" '*Outside-the-World*,' " breathed Dmu Dran faintly, a strange expression on his gaunt skull face, one that mingled unholy loathing with unholy rapture.

"What does it mean, Outside-the-World?" asked the desert prince.

"I don't know," admitted Doc. "I honestly don't know."

Zarouk turned to stare at the strange portal. He rapped it gingerly with the end of the handle of his torch. It made a muffled, thudding sound.

"It doesn't sound hollow, lord," whispered Houm, hesitantly. "How does it open, then?"

"I don't know, fool," snapped Zarouk, eyes glittering with wild fires in the glare of the torches. "But this is the thing we came to find, nonetheless. This is the Door to Zhiam—and we have the key to it!"

The fat merchant opened his mouth to ask another question, but remained silent when he saw the look on

Zarouk's face. He was taut and quivering, and in this mood it was not wise to incur his wrath.

"So *that's* what 'Zhiam' means, eh?" muttered Ryker to Doc. "All this time, I been thinkin' it was a name, not a word—"

"Yes," the old man murmured. "The dialect is so ancient the words don't sound like the language as spoken today. I knew it meant 'Outside,' sure. But I thought that was, well, you know . . . a reference to the fact that the land the Lost Nation got to was outside the areas of Mars the Nine Clans ruled. But now . . . now, I'm beginning to wonder. . . ."

"How's that?"

"I mean, look, my boy, what I said about no caverns being possible in this sort of soil still goes. Why, we couldn't even be standing down here in this big room, if it wasn't for all those metal girders bracing the walls and roof."

"But, hell, Doc!" grunted Ryker bewilderedly. "Where else could the door lead, otherwise?"

"I . . . don't know. I hardly dare try to guess! But remember one thing, my boy—the Old Race were masters of a strange science beyond even our present level of knowledge. You've seen the so-called 'thought-records' they left, we got 'em in museums today. Recorded thought-waves, imperishably stamped in pure metal! No idea how they did it. And other things as well—fragments of machinery with no moving parts, just geometrically-shaped pieces of crystal somehow impregnated with electromagnetic energy—'course they don't work anymore, the machines. But we couldn't duplicate 'em if we tried."

"So—'Outside-the World'?"

"Don't even try to guess," whispered Doc. " 'Cause we're about the find out—"

He pointed. Ryker turned to look.

The priest had taken out the replica of the Keystone which Ryker had carved under the drug-induced trance.

Now, as Zarouk and the warriors shrank back, mumbling half-forgotten boyhood prayers, Dmu Dran stepped forward.

He pressed the Keystone against the very center of the huge disk of blue-green alloy.

He pressed the rounded side against the metal first.

Nothing at all happened.

Then he reversed the Keystone with trembling hands, and set the flat side against it, the side with the odd, geometrical symbolic inscription cut into the slick stone.

He tried the stone first horizontal, then with the larger, more rounded end pointing directly up.

A shiver of awe ran through the thronged warriors.

Then they cried out!

*The panel melted away into a spangled, glittering mist.*

Motes of quivering indigo and emerald dust swirled queerly, revealing a round, circular opening cut into the dry stone.

The motes swam in a weaving, spiral motion, like the Brownian motion of dust suspended in a liquid.

Through the opening in the wall fell a weird golden light.

A wind blew upon their faces, heady, perfumed, and— strangest of all on this desert world—*moist!*

*The Door to Outside was open.*

# IV
## Outside the World

## 16. Strange Eden

BEYOND THE DOOR the desert warriors found a weird new world, a world such as they had never envisioned, even in their most phantasmagoric dreams.

It was the air that seemed uncanniest to them, at first.

It was moist and warm, and redolent of growing things, rich with a curious perfumed sweetness, like delectable spices, whose nature they could not identify.

But Ryker could. He leaned against the rock wall and drank the warm, intoxicating fragrance deeply into his lungs. He remembered his boyhood, and his eyes misted . . . a small, two-story white frame house on the outskirts of Reno, Nevada, with a picket fence and a tall tree in the front yard . . . a smiling woman in a checkered apron, calling his name in a voice that was scarcely a memory to him any more, and himself answering in a childish treble- . . . bare legs with scabs on the knees from falling down, and well-worn sneakers . . . and a small, scruffy, black-and-white dog yapping at his heels as he ran to the house, a dog long forgotten, save in dreams . . . and, by the door, the small, sturdy figure that had once been himself, pausing before a bush of green, glossy leaves where white blossoms grew, inhaling the sweet, spicy fragrance . . .

He blinked back sudden tears.

The scent that puzzled the Martians was familiar to him.

It was the scent of flowers.

● ● ●

For a time they stood about, or wandered idly, like men in a daze of dreams.

Everything they saw about them was new and strange and wonderful, and full of beauty.

From the round mouth of the door stretched a thick, dewy sward of strange, soft, cushiony moss, deep metallic indigo starred with minute white flowers. Beyond grew thick, rustling bushes, swaying in the scented breezes. And then a stand of—trees?—something very like them, at any rate. To Ryker's dazed vision they resembled towering stalks of raw celery, somehow grown to Brobdingnagian proportions, and fronded with feathery plumes of azure.

Something fluttered in the hazy air, and went past them on flickering . . . wings? Yes, wings, on a world where birds or butterflies have never flown. Ryker shielded his gaze from the golden glare of the skies, and peered after the flying thing, hardly daring to believe what he saw.

It was neither bird nor insect, but—a serpent! A slim, graceful, undulant form, rose pink, and flecked with gem-like scales, its wedge-shaped head oddly crested with a fierce violet cockscomb—a serpent in every detail, save that it flew on wings like feathery, transparent sprays of membranous opal.

Someone stumbled into him from behind and he turned to see Doc bent over, fingering the queer bushes, mumbling entrancedly to himself. The old man seemed lost in a dream.

The golden glare from above, which he had glimpsed when the winged serpent fluttered by, caught his wandering attention then, and Ryker looked up.

He could not have said what he thought he might see—a rocky cavern roof far overhead, perhaps—but whatever he had expected, he didn't see it. Instead he saw a vast, fathomless reach of the firmament, filled with pale golden fire and streaked with long thin filaments of—cloud?—oddly pinkish green, at any rate, and curiously regular in shape, with a gelatinous, near-solid look to them. But he was almost beyond wonderment by now, and merely drank in the sky of luminous gold without thinking about it.

At the zenith hung a disk of brilliant white fire. It seemed about the same size as the sun was, seen from the Martian surface, but intolerably more radiant, and lacking the yellowish tinge of the sun he had always known. This new sun was white and fierce, and younger than the sun he knew.

He wandered off into a grove of peculiar trees. They had long, graceful, drooping fronds, like an earthly willow, except that the fronds were each one long feathery leaf, like a palm, but rich metallic indigo. And there was no trunk to these feather trees, the frond sprang from one branch, and the stem of each branch was separate, although they all grew in a clump.

Ryker had never seen or heard of trees like these.

Nor the bushes that grew thick between them, either.

They were a paler shade of blue, and had glossy leaves like enormous ferns. But ferns grown waist high, and from a thick central stem.

He wandered on, and presently he came to the source of the sweet, spicy perfume.

The flowers grew as large as the head of an adult man, and were gauze thin, delicate as tissue. Translucent they were; pale gossamer petals colored the vague, changing hues of opals. And they were as fragile to the touch as they looked. He touched one, rubbed its petals gently between his fingers—and the enormous, frail blossom vanished like a soap-bubble, leaving a sweet-scented residue on his fingers, like a drop of fragrant essence.

But he was beyond marvel now.

At least he thought he was.

He strolled on, drinking in the sweet, moist, warm air, shedding his thermalsuit with an absent gesture, no longer needing it to shield him from the cold, dry bite of the thin Martian air.

For he was no longer on Mars.

He knew this for certain when he came to the pool. A natural pond of water, open to the sky, was unknown on the desert world. Back on the Mars he knew it would have evaporated like a puff of steam, in mere instants of time.

But not here, evidently.

He stared at it, wonderingly.

For here one was: a pool of sweet, cold, fresh water bubbling up from hidden springs. Several of the desert warriors knelt beside the pool, like men in a trance, hardly daring to believe the evidence of their eyes. One gingerly dipped a dusty finger in the limpid water, and sucked it, a dazed expression in his eyes.

One by one the others bent and drank. Never in all their lives had they seen a pool of water before. They hardly knew what to make of it.

Glossy-leafed bushes rustled then, and a sinuous, furry form glided into view and stood watching them from huge, unwinking eyes like luminous amber or topaz. Ryker froze. So did the warriors, none of whom had ever seen such a creature before.

It looked very much like a cat, but it was larger than a cheetah, its slim, graceful body clad in sleek, gleaming fur, coppery red. It had enormous, prick-eyes, fragile, silken and oval, lambent eyes that glowed in its elfin, heart-shaped face. It was impossibly beautiful.

The cat creature paid no particular attention to them, after that first long, enigmatic stare. It stretched indifferently, yawned, revealing a dainty pink tongue, and ambled away to stretch out on the azure moss beneath the nearest tree. It was not only unafraid of them, it didn't seem to find them particularly interesting.

There sounded a dull *plop,* and a plump, golden fruit fell to the cushioning moss near the cat creature. The feline yawned again, sniffed the fruit lazily, and began to devour it daintily.

Then a small furry rodentlike animal came wriggling up from the moss to investigate the bits of fruit the cat had let fall.

The newcomer was about the size of a rabbit, with silky fur, pale blue, and pink eyes and white whiskers and a wriggling pink nose. It looked like a fat mouse.

The cat completely ignored it, after one sideways glance. Then it let the rind of the fruit fall to the ground and began lazily to groom its whiskers with one velvet paw. At its feet, utterly fearless, the fat blue rodent began nibbling at the remnants of the fruit. Ryker could hardly believe his eyes.

Beside him Doc appeared, observing this most curiously *un*feline behavior. The old man mumbled something under his breath in what sounded like Hebrew.

"Eh?" murmured Ryker.

The old man blinked at him, then grinned, flushing a little.

"Sorry! I will translate." His eyes grew dreamy. " 'And the Lord God planted a garden eastwards in Eden. . . .' "

Ryker nodded, his eyes thoughtful. "I know what you mean, Doc. Do you remember the rest of it?"

"Like I know my own hand," the old man said softly.

"Let me think . . . yes . . . 'And God said, "Behold, I have given you every plant yielding seed which is upon the face of the Earth, and every tree with seed in its fruit; you shall have them for food. And to every beast of the earth, everything that has the breath of life, I have given every green plant for food." And it was so. And God looked upon his handiwork, and saw that it was good.' "

The words stirred up old, long-forgotten memories within Ryker. He thought of that white frame house, and its little garden, and the small black and white dog, and the smiling woman who had once read to him these same words from an old, old book.

"Eden, eh?" he murmured. "And is there a Serpent in it yet, I wonder?"

Doc looked behind them to where Zarouk was striding about, yelling, rousing his men from their dreams, marshalling them into battle formation.

"Yes, there is," he whispered somberly. "And, God help us, I think it is you and I, my boy, who have let the Serpent in."

*And the evening and the morning were the sixth day.*

## 17. The Dreaming City

IT TOOK A long time and much yelling for Zarouk to bring his men out of their trance and into order. When at last this was done, he led them down the gentle slope and into the strange new world they had found beyond the door.

As for the door itself, they left it open. Indeed, they were not entirely sure how to close it, even with the Keystone. The spangled mist of blue-green motes into which the Martium panel had vaporized remained in its immaterial state, a curtain of metallic haze drawn across the round opening in the rock of the low red cliff. Zarouk guessed it would stay that way until the Keystone returned the vapor to its solid form.

Ryker figured Zarouk thought it wise to leave the escape route open, in case they needed it. For there was no telling how terribly, and with what unguessable weapons of scientific wizardry, the devil worshippers would be armed.

As they marched down into the vast, dreaming valley which lay open before them under the golden sky, Ryker was not so sure about those weapons. This gentle garden world did indeed seem like a very Eden—where even the lion would lie down with the lamb, and cats did not eat mice, but fed on lush ripe fruit instead.

Did they have war here, too? He found it difficult to imagine. This uncanny Eden seemed gentle, defenseless. He could not believe that men needed weapons here.

Zarouk had brought his weapons with him, of course. And he would use them.

In the broad valley below they found the City.

It was built upon many waters. Lakes and canals surrounded it, and lush gardens and parks.

But it was walled, as all the Martian cities were, walled with clear, glistening marble, pale golden, and lucent as alabaster.

At the sight of it, Doc stopped short with a gasp. Curious emotion lit his eyes, a dawning comprehension, and a dawning wonderment as if he now envisioned some marvel transcending even those they had already seen.

But when Ryker asked him, he only shook his head.

"Later, later, my boy—when I'm sure," was all he would say.

In truth, it was very beautiful, the City. It was built according to the immemorial Martian mode, walled courts and dome-roofed houses, slender minarets and long colonnades, with a central square, and a palace that fronted thereupon, and a huge square structure like a temple, too, and the streets radiated out from the central square like the spokes of the wheel.

The roofs were red tiled, and the houses had lush gardens, and canals meandered through the City, here and there, arched by little bridges. Men and women poled through those waterways in narrow boats with graceful, upcurved prows, like the gondolas of Venice.

There was only one gate to the City, and it was shut and barred.

But there were no guards before the gate, and no warriors stationed upon the walls. And that was very strange, indeed. Were these people so terribly armed with ancient weapons of science or magic, that they had no need of swords and spears?

Perhaps. The possibility was frightening.

Zarouk made his camp before the entrance of the broad causeway that arched over a lake to end before the gate of the City. His men reared their tents and made their fires and began to scout for food. They found the cat beasts marvelously easy to hunt, and easier yet to slay.

The creatures seemed not to comprehend what was being done to them. They would stand gazing indifferently at the hunters who tried to creep up on them, but they neither tried to dodge or flee when the darts flew or the spears struck.

Ryker saw one beautiful red cat pinned to the moss by spears, but still living. As the hunters came up to cut its throat the beast regarded them with puzzled eyes, stretching out a gentle paw as if to touch them. It just had time to utter one plaintive, questioning mew before they cut its throat.

Ryker found the slaughter of these gentle, fearless, puzzled creatures sickening. That night he and the scientist ate dried meat and bread brought with them from Mars, for to have eaten of the cat creatures, they would have had to be a lot hungrier than they were.

"Oh, we have let the Serpent into Eden all right," sighed Herzog. "You saw it yourself, my boy. The cats had never been hunted before, no. They didn't even know what was happening. They—I think they thought maybe the men wanted to—to *play*. . . ."

And Ryker felt sicker than before.

He began to wish they had killed him before he had made the replica of the stone seal. But it was too late for recriminations now.

●　●　●

The strange white sun-star of this world sank in a sunset sky the color of tangerine and the long filaments of cloud were painted vermilion and magenta.

Ryker sat on a log before his tent looking at the City.

He hadn't known what to expect of Zhiam. But a city of devil worshippers had no right to be this serene and cool and beautiful. The ugliness, the perversion of its people, their dedication to evil, should have shown in their handiwork, somehow.

But the City was a dream of fragile beauty, slim towers floating against the dying fires of the sun, domes like ripe fruit or the breasts of women seeming to float like enormous bubbles upon the waters. . . .

No, there was no evil in the City men called Outside.

But—in its people?

It was hard to hazard a guess. It was the orothodox Martians who called them *zhaggua*—worshippers of devils. He had yet to hear Valarda's side of the story.

But then his heart hardened and his face grew grim. Beautiful or not, this was Valarda's kingdom. and she had lied to him, fooled him, tricked him, cheated him, robbed him, left him to die, bound and helpless, among his enemies.

There was no doubt about *that*.


The City knew they were there, but paid no attention. No flags flew, no bugles were blown, no warriors gathered to the defense of Zhiam.

The City dreamed in the dim moonlight, under the glitter of ten thousand stars.

There were fewer stars blazing in this sky of nights than made splendid the nighted skies of Mars. But, like Mars, this planet also had twin moons, one larger than the other.

140

The moons of Mars, Deimos and Phobos, were too small and too low in albedo to be clearly visible even at night. In fact, they were all but impossible to see with the unaided eye. You had to know exactly where they were in the sky to glimpse them at all.

But here the moons, although small, were visible, disks of pallid silver against dark purple velvet.

The desert men ignored the splendor of the skies. They were not made for this warmth and humidity, and the air of this planet was so rich in oxygen, compared to what they had known, that its headiness intoxicated them. They perspired greasily, stripped to mere loincloths, panting breathlessly in what seemed to them an unendurably tropical heat.

To Ryker and his companion, the night was mild and balmy. Both Earthlings had gone through the series of treatments that readjusted their body chemistries to conditions on Mars. But this did not mean they could not readjust to conditions more like those on Earth. Their organic modifications reacted like thermostats to whatever conditions they found themselves in. So they, at least, were comfortable.

Doc seemed utterly fascinated by the spectacle of the skies. The constellations were strange and new to both of them, of course and, although he said nothing, Ryker guessed the scientist was trying to find a signpost in the altered constellations which might indicate their position in the universe.

In this he guessed wrong, as things turned out.

"Doc, you aren't gonna find any stars you recognize," Ryker argued. "We're in another dimension, aren't we?"

The Israeli savant snorted through his nose, rudely.

"My boy, when you don't know what you're talking about, then shut up," he said. "The only dimensions you got to worry about are length, breadth and thickness.''

''What about the fourth dimension?''

''Duration. And it's not really a dimension like the others, it's a condition for existence. To exist at all, a thing has to have length, breadth and thickness—and it has to endure for a measurable unit of time. They been misquoting Einstein for two hundred years, it's time they stopped. So stop, already!''

Ryker grinned and shut up. Doc could be cantankerous at times, especially when you interrupted him during a bout of cogitation.

But he couldn't help wondering what Doc was cogitating about. He gave it up and turned in to sleep. Doc would tell him when he was ready to, and not one moment before.

The night was so balmy he couldn't endure the notion of wrapping himself up in the fleece-lined sleeping cloak of *orthavva* fur, so he simply stretched out on the cool, dewy moss and slept in the raw.

In the morning the assault on Zhiam would begin, he knew.

Despite his thirst for revenge, he wasn't looking forward to it.


Zarouk was up before dawn, rousting his men from their hot, untidy slumbers—for they had slept in the furs, as they were accustomed to sleeping—and preparing for the assault.

The advance unit marched across the causeway to the closed gate, without being attacked from above. Neither spear nor dart was let fall upon them from above. And the walls indeed seemed unattended.

They marched back, feeling foolish.

Two squads were sent back into the forest to cut down the trees so that Xinga's team could construct rams and scaling ladders. And all the time the City lay dreaming beneath the radiance of dawn, serene and untroubled, scarcely deigning to notice them.

Before noon, they attacked the walls. The ladders went up and the ram team assaulted the gates of the City. They were of bronze, and rang beneath the beaten blows like a mighty gong.

Strange figures appeared atop the walls, and, at first, Zarouk grinned at the sight of them. It was a relief to be no longer ignored; it had been as if their force was so neglible that the men of the City were indifferent to it. Now, at last, the defenders of Zhiam had come forth.

But they were strange defenders.

Darts glanced off them, tinkling to fragments, without causing them any discomfort. Their bodies were curiously thick and sheathed in some odd crystalline white substance which hid even their faces.

They carried no weapons at all.

Ignoring the rain of darts—ignoring the heavy, metal-shod spears—they confined their activities to throwing the ladders back off the walls, one by one. Men fell, squalling, from the toppling ladders, and the ones who were lucky landed in the moatlike lake before the gate. The unlucky ones fell in the bushes or on the mossy ground, to their considerable detriment. There were broken legs aplenty, and more than a few men fell on their heads.

The ladders were raised again—and again—and again —by the dozens. But the strange armored men threw them down every time. They seemed utterly impervious to the darts, even to the darts tipped with the nerve poison the Martians distill from venom, and the heavy spears ricochetted from their breasts or heads or shoulders without even staggering them.

Zarouk was baffled, and getting angry. He sent a team out armed with lassos made of leather thongs, to capture one of the warriors on the wall.

*It was a man-shaped statue of living stone.*

The desert men shrank back from the uncanny thing, hissing in superstitious terror. Even Zarouk blanched and recoiled from it, shuddering.

It was rather roughly hewn from some strange, sparkling white stone, hard and crystalline, resembling quartz. Its hands were shaped like crude mittens, and its face was devoid of any features whatsoever, not even eyes.

And it really was entirely made of solid stone.

Yet it lived, and moved.

Ryker stared with fascination as the stone giant writhed slowly, straining against its bonds until they snapped and broke. The places where elbows or knees would have been on something human, the stone seemed to suddenly soften—the joints became viscous—when the limb was about to flex. As soon as the limb had moved, the stone hardened again.

A head and a half taller than the tallest of the warriors, the stone colossus got clumsily to its feet and began ponderously to stride back towards the City.

The men shrank from it fearfully, but it ignored them.

Xinga turned questioning eyes on his master, and hefted a lasso tentatively.

"No, let it go," muttered Zarouk. "How do you kill a thing that isn't really alive? Let it go."

The walking statue crossed the causeway, approaching the gate. Then it began to climb, using the ornate carvings around the gate for stepping-stones. It fell twice and climbed back each time unhurt before it gained the top of the walls again.

Zarouk watched with hating eyes, while the City dreamed on, indifferent to anything he might bring against it.

## · 18. The Winged Serpents

ZAROUK WAS IN a furious rage, and Houm carefully avoided his company in so far as he was able. Even Xinga thought it most prudent to busy himself with certain tasks which precluded his personal attendance on his prince.

Zhiam seemed quite adequately defended by the Stone Giants, and any further attempts to storm the walls by ladder appeared hopeless of success. Nevertheless two more such forays were launched during the night, under the cover of darkness.

At four widely separated points about the walls of the City, assault squadrons, muffled in dark robes and careful to avoid excessive noise, stole in secret to the foot of the ramparts and sought to scale the battlements without being discovered.

The night was heavily overcast with clouds, and was probably as dark as ever nights were on this strange world. However, despite the furtive and stealthy nature of the attack, it was a dismal failure.

The Stone Giants, as they had done before, simply threw the ladders down from the walls, and the men who were ascending them fell squalling lustily. Then, gathering up their dead and injured, and retrieving the ladders, they limped away and returned to camp to report to their scowling master.

Evidently, the Stone Giants had senses that could perceive the approach of dangerous enemies even in the moonless, starless gloom. Also, they seemingly patrolled the ramparts by day and by night, which was, thought Ryker, only to be expected. Men fashioned of lifeless stone, who were invulnerable to injury, also should be impervious to weariness or fatigue, and—not actually being living creatures, save in a technical sense—did not ever require sleep.

None of this did anything to improve the ferocious temper of the Desert Hawk.

The following day, Zarouk made a tour of the outer works of the Dreaming City, and rode the circuit of the walls, looking for weaknesses. He was forced to ford the streams and canals, and to ride about the small lake, but otherwise he examined every yard of the perimeter, finding no loopholes in the defenses of Zhiam.

There was only one gate, and it was of solid metal. While it might prove possible to break in through this portal by the employment of rams, that would take considerable time. The City had no other gates, not even a small postern gate.

The stone ramparts completely encircled the metropolis of the Lost Nation, and were of equal height at every point. And during his tour of the defenses, Zarouk counted no fewer than sixty of the Stone Giants maintaining their constant and imperturbable vigilance.

Unless he could manage it so that his warriors attacked the wall at more than sixty points, it did not seem possible for them to successfully assault the barricades. And such was the length of the wall and the size of the City itself, that even were he to mount such an attack, the Stone Giants would still be near enough to the unprotected portions to reach them in time to prevent any of the desert raiders from reaching the crest of the walls.

And, besides, to attempt to attack the ramparts simultaneously in more than sixty places was numerically impossible. Zarouk did not have enough men with him to mount such an attack effectively.

Even it it was possible for him to get a few men atop the wall, they would be useless against the unkillable defenders. None of their weapons could inflict upon the Giants an injury sufficient to disable them.

For that he would need power guns. And Zarouk had no power guns.

It looked like stalemate.

Later that day, Zarouk sent his warriors against the gate in full strength. The trees in the forest did not make the best rams imaginable, but they were all Zarouk had to work with and would have to do. Back on Mars, his raiders would have used stone pillars slung by chains from heavy braces for this purpose. Here it was still probably possible to find such resources in a quarry or outcropping, but he lacked the tools to chip or cut lengths of stone into the proper proportions.

For an hour or two his men toiled away against that portal of solid metal, finding it unyielding. The Stone Giants, or some of them at any rate, gathered atop the wall at the gate to observe the attack, but made no effort to injure the men who toiled below.

This was in itself curious. Surely, they could have striven to discourage the ram teams with spears or darts. Lacking these, they could have emptied cauldrons of boiling water or burning oil upon the men below. But none of these actions were undertaken by the stone colossi, who seemed content merely to observe the labor of the invaders.

It was as if, for some reason, they were forbidden to kill, and could only repulse an attack, not initiate one.

Ryker thought this was very queer.

After an hour or two of this, a few human observers appeared atop the battlements to watch the rams. One of these was a frail old man with a silver furcap, his lean body wrapped in gorgeous brocades. Ryker recognized him as Melandron.

*Another was Valarda herself.*

She was dressed like an empress, her slim golden body blazing with gems and precious metals, draped in rich fabrics. The black silk of her hair was caught in a net studded with winking purple rubies, and atop her proud head she wore a construction of curving gold loops and arabesques like a crown. From a clip of strange amber gems fixed to the browpiece of this odd-shaped coronet, glossy plumes of pink and peach and pistachio green floated behind her. Her small, firm breasts were cupped in shallow coils of golden wire.

He stared at her hungrily, his eyes slitted and hard and hating. She leaned over the parapet to observe the activity below, then turned her face to make some remark to a smooth-faced young princeling who stood beside her. Evidently, it was a jest, because he laughed and she smiled.

Then she looked down again and across the length of the causeway, and her eyes met those of Ryker.

She knew him in an instant, and her face went pale. Suddenly her great eyes became shadowed, her face drawn and somehow mournful. She said nothing, and made no sign, but looked at him for a long time with an expression on her perfect features that resembled sorrow.

Fat Houm had spied her as well, and sidled up to where Zarouk stood overseeing the toiling of the men at the rams. The greedy merchant whispered in Zarouk's ear and drew his attention to the slim, graceful golden girl on the ramparts.

He barked an order, and his guards lifted to their lips the long black tubes they used with such deadly accuracy as blowguns.

Ryker stepped forward uncertainly, his lips shaping a cry which he never spoke—

The languid handsome youth beside Valarda saw all of this in the same instant. Languidly he raised to his own lips a long, slim-throated horn of glittering gold. A sharp liquid song pierced the air, shrilly calling. A beckoning sound, emphatic as a regal summons, rang forth.

*Suddenly the air was filled with winged serpents.*

Sleek, jewelled coils drifting and undulating on the air, upheld by the thrumming of those strange wings like fans of thick plumes, they darted about like hummingbirds.

Ryker watched the first of Zarouk's marksmen loose the first of the poisoned darts.

A serpent plucked it from midair!

Then a veritable shower of the slim, deadly needles flew from the mouths of the black tubes. Not so much as one of these reached its mark.

The men lowered their tubes, grimacing lamely.

The golden horn sang forth again, a keen, peremptory command composed of three liquid notes.

The writhing cloud of airborne serpents who floated before Valarda to shield her from the darts, now flung themselves down upon the marksmen.

The men wavered, broke, fled in all directions, pursued by agile and flickering wings.

The serpents caught in their fanged mouths the slim black tubes and bore them away.

Then the aerial swarm turned its attentions upon the ram teams, in instantaneous response to a trilling of the golden horn.

Swarming in midair above the apprehensive warriors,

they darted down to snap fanged jaws before the faces of the fearful warriors, who threw their hands before their eyes to protect them from the darting serpents.

They darted hither and thither—hovered to beat their plumes in the faces of the warriors—arrowed in writhing flights to snatch at their cloaks—buffeting them about the head and neck with beating wings—virtually snapping at their heels like a pack of mongrels.

The men blanched, threw down their rams, and ran for shelter.

The aerial serpents pursued them back to their camp, then rose in a twisting stream of glittering pink-and-azure forms, and floated back to the parapets.

While Ryker and the men near him stared in awe, Valarda laughed, caressing the graceful creatures as if to thank them. They fluttered away behind the walls, vanishing from view, but probably they did not go far and could be summoned again, swiftly and easily.

Then the Stone Giants dropped lines over the lip of the parapet, snagged several of the makeshift rams in the sharp teeth of the hooked grapnels affixed to the ends of the lines, and dragged about half of the beams up to the top of the walls.

The workers growled and grimaced and waved threatening fists, but none of them quite dared risk another attack by the flying snakes to return to the foot of the wall in order to retrieve the rams they had abandoned.

Zarouk vanished into his tent, his brow thunderous.

And it was still stalemate. In fact, now it was even more so.

The human inhabitants of the City lingered for a little while atop the battlements as if waiting for more action to commence. Finally, they drifted off lazily, vanishing from sight.

Valarda was the last to leave, and before she too turned to go she looked again at Ryker. Her face was sad and her eyes seemed eloquent and pleading. Then she sighed, and vanished from his view.

That evening he lay a long time under the misty skies, staring at nothing. His thoughts were disordered, his emotions in turmoil. If Valarda had laughed at him, mocked him, spurned him, he would have been easier in his heart.

But she had not. She had seemed to beg him wordlessly for forgiveness. And that he could not forget.

He had assumed her his enemy, and had hated her, despising himself for the ache of desire he still felt in his loins for the golden girl.

And he had accepted without quarrel or dispute the black and dire assessment of Zarouk upon the folk of Zhiam. The desert prince called them devil worshippers, and so Ryker had thought of them.

But could men who worship evil have raised so lovely a dream city as this?

Could such evil dwell in this Edenic garden world, among such exquisite loveliness?

Could horror find a home here, where even the beasts did not eat of each others' flesh, but fed from ripe fruits, side by side, the lion lying down with the lamb?

Ryker was beginning, however reluctantly, to change his opinion of the Lost Nation. Despite what Zarouk and men like him said of this people, they appeared to be a serene and peaceful race, lovers of beauty, who lived in tranquility, and existed in harmony with this calm and lovely world they had found.

It seemed beyond dispute that this was true. The tales he had been told of the despicable *zhaggua* and their evil ways perhaps were sullied and distorted by the blind

152

fanaticism of men like the priest Dmu Dran, and by the cunning of such ambitious zealots as Zarouk, and by the greed of such as Houm. And those tales might not be true.

Why had not Valarda unleashed against them the immensely strong Stone Giants, to slay and maim the warriors?

Why had not the warriors of her own people manned the walls, to cut the desert raiders down with spear and dart and missile?

*Why had not the winged serpents so much as inflicted a single wound upon the men when they harried them from the gate?*

If this world was truly another Eden, then perchance its unknown and nameless god had issued forth a commandment which was to be obeyed by all of the living creatures of this world, including men—a commandment identical to another given voice by yet a different God from the cloud-wrapped heights of Sinai long ago—

*Thou shalt not kill.*

Ryker felt a cold horror growing in his guts. It was he alone had made it possible for these warriors to invade this gentle, idyllic Eden. He had given them the key to open those gates that should have been guarded by angels with flaming swords.

Oh, God, *what had he done?*

# 19. The Secret of Zhiam

RYKER AWOKE SHORTLY before dawn, disturbed by something entering the tent. He sat up swiftly, reaching about him for a weapon. Then he relaxed, leaning back. By the flickering green nightlight of the small bronze pan of liquid fire he saw that it was the old Israeli scientist.

"You're still awake, my boy?" asked the old man in his querulous voice. Ryker nodded, then looked closely at him. Herzog seemed like a man walking in his sleep—distracted, bemused, almost ecstatic.

"Are you all right, Doc?" he asked.

The old man looked at him with eyes filled with excitement.

"What's with me?" he chuckled. "Ah, my boy, you should ask it. I have the proof now, all I need. Wonderful—incredible! You wouldn't believe it!"

"What wouldn't I believe?" grinned Ryker. The old man's enthusiasm could be infectious at times. Ryker didn't know very much about science, and cared little, but the way the scientist was carrying on was beginning to arouse his curiosity. He seemed to be repressing his emotions with difficulty, trembling with sheer delight.

"*I know where we are*—that's all!" Herzog burst out.

Ryker blinked.

"All right, where *are* we?" he asked, as it was obviously expected of him.

Doc sat down, squatting tailor-fashion on a bit of rug one of the warriors had given them for their tent.

"You were thinking it was another dimension," the old man began. "And I told you that it wasn't, because the word doesn't *mean* anything, not in that context, anyway—"

"Yeah," said Ryker flatly. "I remember. Go on."

"Oh, I guessed it from the very beginning! I had no proof, is all. Theories, sure; hypotheses, plenty. But *evidence?* Hard facts, data, these were what I needed. You see, a theory is nothing unless it covers the observed phenomena and accounts for all items of data—"

"*Will* you get to it," groaned Ryker. "Save the lectures for the classroom, just out with it and let me get back to sleep!"

Doc looked apologetic.

"The stars," he blurted. "The constellations were, well, twisted around, maybe, but I could still recognize them. You see, that meant we were still in our galaxy, still in our own immediate stellar neighborhood, in fact. Our system belongs to a—what do you call it in English, outcropping? No—peninsula? Well, whatever. It's called the Orion Spur, and it sticks out of the Carina-Cygnus Arm of our galactic spiral like . . ."

Doc broke off, realizing that he was rambling on in the general direction of another digression. He frowned determinedly. "All right, all right! Here's the gist of it. The constellations were distorted, but not distorted *right*. I mean, they weren't angled around as if we were seeing them from a different direction, or anything like that. They looked inside out, and the only way I could explain *that* was with one single assumption. But it was even more fantastic, the assumption, you see, than the idea that by going through the door we had somehow been transported to another planet somewhere in 'near space.' So I looked around, and believe me, I kept my eyes open!"

Ryker opened his mouth, weary of this roundabout way of getting to the point. Doc raised his hand and hastened to it.

"The cats," he breathed faintly. "There were cats like that back on Mars once, we know, from fossils. In fact, some authorities consider it at least possible that the Martian natives evolved from a common feline ancestry, just like you and I, my boy, evolved from a *simian* ancestor. But there are no apes on Mars, and nothing like apes, and there never have been."

He grinned excitedly, his face lighting up with enthusiasm.

"And then, those *trees*," he burbled. "Well, there used to be trees of some sort back on Mars, too, and again we know this from the fossil record."

An uncanny presentiment began to make Ryker's nape hairs lift, and the skin creep on his forearms.

"Doc, what are you trying to say?" he breathed.

"And the vegetation is all *blue!* Just like it is on Mars, even today! Oh, biochemists worked out the formula for photosynthesis on Mars way back when. With the kind of sunlight that reaches Mars, blue vegetation can photosynthesize just as well as green does back where you and I come from. You know? But trees—and those cats—and air this warm and humid, and all the free water in those lakes—Mars hasn't had any of these things in millions and millions of years! So that was the problem I sort of had to solve. Oh, I knew the answer already, by sheer intuition; but the solution to the problem was even more fantastic than the problem itself, if you know what I mean. But I put the facts together, and they *fit*—"

"Where—"

"So, where are we, you ask?" The aged scientist

beamed upon him fondly. "On Mars, my boy, where else?"

"But—" began Ryker, exasperatedly.

"The important question isn't really *where*," finished Doc. "It's—*when!*"

Ryker blinked at him dazedly.

"You mean, when we stepped through the Door to Zhiam, we didn't travel through space at all, but through—*time?*"

Herzog nodded affably.

Ryker looked at him, incredulously. But a dawning comprehension filled his mind. Suddenly, all sorts of curious facts and observations, scraps and bits and pieces, began to fall together. And they made a kind of sense.

*The peculiar expression on the faces of Valarda and Melandron when they looked for the first time upon the Lost City—that expression of mingled sorrow and horror. The city had been fresh and new when last they had seen it—they or their ancestors, that is—now it was crumbling into ruin.*

*The unknown language in which they had at times conversed—an obsolete variant of the modern Tongue, elsewhere but in Zhiam forgotten for ages.*

*The golden eyes of the girl—strange color that has not been seen in the eyes of Martians for many ages.*

*The very name of the old man, Melandron, like something out of one of the ancient sagas.*

It all fit together perfectly. Even the fact that they permitted him to go with them. It was as if they did not share the contemporary Martian prejudice against the Earthsider colonists who had raped, despoiled and seized their world. *To them he was only an interesting curiosity.* They had not lived through the grim horrors of CA occu-

157

pation, watching their land taken over by aliens, their men enslaved, their women ravished and cast aside—*they had perhaps never even seen an Earthling before.*

"How—far—back?" he asked hoarsely.

Doc shrugged carelessly.

"A billion years, maybe. Maybe two billion. Hard to say. The movements of the stars into what we know as the present constellations is a very gradual thing. They all look deformed, out of shape, because they are here and now, I mean moving into the alignments familiar to us. I would say, however—"

But Ryker was no longer listening. His mind echoed and reechoed with that astounding, that enormous, that world-shaking fact.

*Two—billion—years!*

There was no point in wondering how the Lost Nation had accomplished the miracle. Time travel was an old idea. Back on Earth the science fiction writers had played with it for a couple of centuries. Science seemed to agree that it was an impossibility. Time is simply the measure of change, of entropic decay; any reversal of entropy rate would seem to be purely a contradiction in terms.

But science had to adapt to existing facts, or it was as unreliable as theology. This *was* ancient Mars, beyond all question. That fierce white sun was the old familiar sun, as it looked aeons earlier in time. Those curious feather trees were known from their fossilized remains. So, too, with the great cats; extinct for many ages, they were considered by some to be the evolutionary ancestor of the Martian natives. Those two moons, just barely visible in the night sky, were Deimos and Phobos, the moons of Mars. The blue moss that covered the soil, the blue vegetation, the strange flowers—blue vegetation still existed on the Mars

Ryker knew, but it was scarce and had evolved into simpler, hardier forms over ages of gradual dehydration which had reduced this warm and fertile planet into a dying world of naked rock and bleak dust desert.

It had long been known that the remote ancestors of the Martian people had possessed a highly advanced technology, about which little was known for only a few of their machines or instruments had survived the attrition of time.

*Somehow* they had found a way to open a portal to the distant past, and into that forgotten age they had fled from the persecution of the fanatical priests, to seek a realm where they could live in peace and worship their strange new god according to their own ways.

No wonder that the Keystone was of such vital importance to them, for locked within its black crystal was the power to trigger the portal, to open or to seal the door. And when the unnamed renegade had fled from their ancient Eden, he had left the door . . . ajar.

And through it they had feared the descendants of their old persecutors might pour, to exterminate them as once of old they had been faced with extermination.

And the fear had not been groundless. For their enemies had come—and he, Ryker, had shown them the way!

And now Ryker began to understand why Valarda had left him to die atop the desolate plateau.

She had known that Zarouk's raiders were following at their very heels. And she had the thing she had come into the future to find—the all-important Keystone, which meant life or death for her people in the past.

The decision must have been an agonizing one. She had weighed in the balance the debt she owed the Outworlder for saving her from the mob and for assisting her in her journey home, against the very survival of her nation.

And she had decided that the fate of thousands outweighed one single life.

Ryker wondered if he would have decided it any differently, if he had been in her place, deciding to leave her in order to save his own people.

He hoped he would never have such a terrible decision to make, for he doubted if he could accept the burden of that awful responsibility.

But now he understood why she had done it. And he knew the meaning of that stricken, pleading expression in her eyes when she had stared down at him from the parapet yesterday.

He slept no more that night.

Zarouk was up with dawn with a new idea for assaulting the walls of Zhiam.

He sent his men back to the grove to cut down some of the limber boughs of the willowlike trees they had seen when first they had entered this place outside the world.

And he began to construct a row of primitive-looking seige engines.

Ryker thought of them as catapults, until Doc corrected him on his terminology.

"No, no, my boy! Catapult is not the proper word at all. A catapult is like a gigantic bow and arrow. What the Prince seems to be building is the sort of thing the ancient Romans would have called a *ballista*. During the Middle Ages, they knew them as mangonels. See the cup-shaped basket at the other end? That's for hurling stones."

Ryker had to admire the Desert Hawk for his resourcefulness. Armed with these engines, the raiders could keep well back from the walls and hurl heavy boulders at the fortifications. The Stone Giants could not bother them, and here the aerial serpents would be out in the open, exposed to darts and spears and blowguns. It was a clever tactic.

By mid-afternoon the first stony missiles began to thump and bang against the gate, which rang like a huge gong when struck. The branches of the feather trees, when lashed together, had just enough ''springiness'' to them to bend down over the crossbars, and to flip the heavy rocks when cut free.

Only the occasional stone actually hit the metal gates. Most of the big stones struck the walls, especially the narrow arch above the portal. Before long the marble would crack and begin to crumble. A couple of days under this sort of bombardment, and the desert raiders would be through the walls and into the City.

A ragged cheer went up lustily from half a hundred throats. One of the great stones had struck a bit high, catching the nearest of the Stone Giants squarely in the chest. The white crystalline stuff of the weirdly animated statue had shattered under the impact, spraying fragments everywhere.

One of the Stone Giants was down, at least, and would never rise again. Zarouk showed his sharp white teeth in a grin like a wolfish leer. It was pleasant to discover that the walking stone men could, after all, be destroyed!

*Thump—thump—clang—crack!*—went the flying boulders as Zarouk kept the wall above the gate under steady bombardment.

It was only a matter of time, Ryker grimly knew.

## 20. The Underground Road

THAT EVENING, AFTER sunset, the encampment of the desert raiders was hit by a surprise attack.

Zarouk planned to keep his men pounding away at the wall with their ballistae throughout the hours of darkness, so as to discourage the dwellers of the City from attempting to effect repairs on the wall.

The folk of the City, however, retaliated in an unsuspected manner.

Suddenly—out of nowhere, it seemed—a large number of the slow, lumbering Stone Giants entered the camp. Impervious to the darts and spears and swords used against them by the startled sentries, they ignored the human warriors and headed straight for the long row of makeshift ballistae.

These they overturned, and began to hammer them apart with balled fists as heavy as stone mauls or hammers.

Zarouk came out of his tent in a fury, thundering commands. He knew very well that it was difficult if not impossible for his warriors to inflict any damage on the animated statues, but they *could* be immobilized, for a time at least, by lassoes.

The sky was clear and the stars twinkled down, and the larger of the twin moons was faintly visible as a ghostly crescent low on the horizon. Lighting the gloom with torches, he sent his lassomen out to rope the ponderous, slow-moving giants.

Before long they managed to snag two of them and pull them off balance, toppling them to the ground. Then, with five or six men pulling at the other end of the rope, they dragged their captives away from the scene and attempted to tie their arms to their bodies with further ropes or thongs. Some of the men were armed with axes or war hammers, and these strove to smash the Stone Giants as the one atop the walls had been broken asunder when hit by the missile.

The other Stone Giants paid no attention to their captive comrades and patiently continued breaking the ballistae apart into fragments.

Like everyone else in the camp, Ryker and the old Israeli had been aroused from their slumbers by the uproar, and came out of their tent to see what was happening.

But unlike the others, who were too busily engaged in trying to immobilize and break up the stone men to have time for curiosity, Ryker wondered just where the Giants had come from, and how they had gotten out of the City. He knew that Zarouk had posted sentries to keep an eye on the gates of the City, so that his camp would *not* be taken by surprise in a foray such as this.

The fact that it *had* been surprised, suggested to Ryker that the Giants had come through the walls by some other entry not as yet discovered.

He imparted this intelligence to the old scientist, who eagerly agreed that it was indeed mysterious. On impulse, the two of them circled the commotion and headed out toward the City, hoping to find out how the Giants had gotten there.

They found the answer to the question with surprising ease, when a portion of the riverbank opened beneath them, quite suddenly, and they fell into a dark, cavernous space.

• • •

Ryker staggered to his feet, limping on a lame leg, blood trickling down into his eyes from a cut on his scalp. The leg did not feel like it was broken, and the rest of him, although bruised and shaken up a bit, was not seriously harmed.

Rubbing the blood out of his eyes, he peered around him in the utter blackness, calling Doc's name in a hoarse voice.

Then he stumbled into something soft and yielding. Dropping to his knees he felt around him with groping hands, encountering the old man's body.

He lay limp and unmoving, but Ryker could hear him breathing and his searching hands found the flutter of a pulse. He ran his hands gently over the old man's limbs, finding that when he touched Herzog's left leg the old man groaned.

A hurt, perhaps broken leg was bad enough. A broken head was worse. And his questing fingers found a lump on the scientist's head the size of a hen's egg. But, anyway, Doc was still alive, and that was something to be thankful for.

His eyes were beginning to adjust to the darkness by now, and some faint starlight was filtering through the hole far above his head. By this dim illumination, he searched the pit into which they had fallen, finding a flight of crude stone steps along one wall leading up to the opening above. By this stair, obviously, the Stone Giants had ascended to the mouth of the pit.

Peering up, he could just make out the details. A sort of double trapdoor made of wooden planks and covered with a natural camouflage of soil and moss had protected the secret entry from discovery. He guessed that the trap had been shut but not barred, left sufficiently ajar so that the

Giants could pry it open and make their escape by this same route, when their work was accomplished. If it had been barred, the chances were that he and Doc could have walked across it without noticing that it was covering a hollowness in the ground, because from the residue of soil and moss which still clung to the trap, he could see that the camouflage had been nearly two feet thick.

Ryker knelt to gather the old man up in his arms, thinking to ascend by the stair and get his companion back to camp, when he was forced to alter his plans.

*The point of a slim rapier was just barely touching the back of Ryker's neck.*

Moving slow and careful, he turned his head to see the smiling features of the slim, languid young lordling who had stood next to Valarda on the parapet, and who had laughed in answer to her jest.

There were five other men with him. And they all wore swords.

And Ryker's hands were empty.

For a moment he simply looked at them. There was no way that he could fight them, here in the dark, in these narrow confines, and lacking any weapon save his bare hands and the iron strength of his burly body.

But he was sorely tempted.

He was sick of being a captive. And these lordlings of Zhiam looked to him slim, delicate, almost effeminate. Their half-naked bodies were silky-smooth, soft—not flabby, but with undeveloped musculature. They looked oddly immature, their smooth cheeks and pointed chins innocent of hair, their bodies slim and effete. *Like boys playing soldier,* he thought sourly to himself.

He did not like their softness, or the gems that twinkled at earlobe and throat and wrist. Instead of the leather tunics and breeches, or long, burnooselike robes usually worn by the warriors of Mars, these dainty princelings went nearly naked—but then, to be fair, in this humid, nigh-tropical climate, there was no need for the heavier raiment common on the Mars he knew.

They wore jewelled girdles of precious metal slung low about their hips, with silken breechclouts of shimmering fabric, the hues of metallic bronze-green, amber, purple or indigo, wound about their slender loins. Bands of gleaming Martium or red-bronze clasped their slim, boyish arms at the biceps and the wrist. Their legs were naked, their feet shod in supple buskins, laced high over the instep.

Their faces were heart shaped as Valarda's, with wide cheekbones, pointed chins, and large, slightly slanted eyes lustrously golden as were hers. They wore their fur caps longer than was the custom among the People he knew, silky russet hair caught in openwork helms made of curved pieces of gold or silver, some adorned with jewels and others haughty with nodding plumes. A few wore short, knee-length cloaks of scarlet cloth—crinkly, shiny-surfaced stuff, like taffeta—and obviously for court fashion rather than for warmth.

He didn't like the looks of them—their soft, underdeveloped bodies, their features so pretty as to verge on girlish beauty, their languid postures, too graceful and affected to be manly. But he had to admit they held their swords expertly enough. They looked as if they knew very well how to use them.

There was no sense in getting himself killed—not here, not like this, like a rat trapped in a black hole in the ground. It would do no good to resist, so he surrendered.

The dainty princeling who had attended Valarda on the parapet murmured some peremptory directive to his retinue. Ryker listened closely this time. Now that he realized the language was an antiquated and obsolete variant of the one universal native language, he thought he could almost catch the sense of what was said.

The pronunciation of the words was oddly different from the Tongue he knew, of course. The phrasing of the remark the princeling drawled to his companions was stilted, archaic and formal, the consonants were spoken with more crispness and sharpness than in the dialect of the Tongue familiar to him, the vowels were rounder and more fully enunciated, rather than being slurred and almost elided, as in the modern forms of speech spoken on the desert world, and some of the verbs were unrecognizable.

But he could catch enough of what the aristocratic personage said to his followers to make out its import.

He said, "Bind this one, and construct a litter for the old man. We shall escort them into Zhiam, since that seems to be their goal. The Priestess will no doubt desire to have words with this ruffian in particular."

So he was a prisoner again!

By now, Ryker was almost getting used to it.

They lashed his wrists behind his back with silken cords which looked flimsy enough, but proved to be surprisingly strong when Ryker surreptitiously tested his strength against them.

It was singularly humiliating to stand there and let these pretty boys tie him up. He towered head and shoulders above most of them, and his arms were bigger around and more heavily muscled than were their thighs. He could have picked them up and tossed them about like dolls, but he bent his head and grimly submitted to being bound.

The Martians took up the limp body of Doc Herzog and

bore it along with them on a makeshift litter fashioned from two slim spears, lashed together with strips torn from one of the crimson cloaks. They treated the injured man gently enough, Ryker saw.

Then, prodded on by their leader, who seemed to be named Lord Thoh, the Zhiamese let Ryker precede them into the tunnel.

It was black as pitch inside, of course, but the flooring was dry and smooth underfoot, and Ryker cautiously felt his way, wary of stumbling over some unseen obstacle in the dark.

The tunnel slanted downwards for a time on a shallow decline, then ran straight for a certain ways, and finally rose to the surface again on a gentle upwards slant.

It had been tunnelled beneath the very bed of the river, he realized, and it was obvious that it was not a recent excavation. Heavy beams of dark azure wood supported the roof at intervals, and crossbraces prevented the earthen walls from crumbling in. The beams were not freshly cut, but old; here and there, they were slick with patches of mold and lichen.

His burly form towering above the slim Zhiamese, Ryker went down into the darkness, feeling rather like Hercules descending into Hades to claim his bride from the King of Shadows. The classical parallel was neat and fitting, but made him feel uncomfortable. One thrust of those slim rapiers, and he would be going down into the Kingdom of Shadows sure enough.

What purpose this underground road had been built to serve, Ryker could not even guess. But he reflected that any city worth its salt has more than one way in—or out.

When they ascended again to the surface of the planet, it was by a stone stair similar to that Ryker had seen at the other end of the subterranean passage. This one gave forth into the interior of a large stone building whose shadowy heights and echoing recesses were brilliantly illuminated by lamps of crystal and some silvery metal. He could have sworn the method of illumination used was fluorescent lighting, but there was no way of telling without examining one of the glowing spheres at close hand.

Here Lord Thoh reported his small triumph to an officer who treated him with the utmost deference, glancing curiously at the tall, rugged Earthling and the unconscious scientist. This officer was manlier and more strongly built than the little party of courtiers, although still an unusually short and slightly built warrior by modern standards. He wore a short tunic of glassy green stuff, covered with shiny scales like some sort of armor, and his helm was of red copper.

Ryker was put into a narrow cell with a barred door and his wrists were cut free.

Then the Zhiamese warriors went away, bearing the unconscious body of the old scientist with them, and Ryker was left alone with his thoughts.

# V
## *An Age That Time Forgot*

## 21. Sentence of Death

THE OFFICER IN charge of the cells was named Aoth. Ryker got to know him a bit. He was gruff but courteous, offering his prisoner no insult, but treating him rather gingerly. Ryker got the idea that the fellow was somewhat in awe of Ryker, curious as to his antecedents—he was obviously not Martian but too polite to ask questions.

He brought Ryker food and drink. The wine was of a superb vintage, heady and effervescent, a pale golden fluid which looked and tasted not unlike champagne. It had been fifteen years since Ryker had last enjoyed a goblet of champagne, and he sipped the beverage appreciatively, thinking that if *this* was the sort of fare served up in the jails of Zhiam, being a prisoner here was not going to be all that tough to endure.

The food was similarly delicious—spicy balls of some reddish meal soaked in hot, succulent sauce, and a sort of hot broth filled with crisp tidbits of herbs and vegetables. It all went down as easily as did the golden wine.

Ryker could not help noticing that there was no meat in his meal. Were these descendants of the ancient Martian rebels all vegetarians, or did their religion prohibit them from slaughtering beasts? If the latter was true, then they seemed a bit too tenderhearted to fit his notion of devil worshippers.

While the cuisine would have done credit to the finest gourmet restaurant, the prison cell was just a prison cell. It boasted nothing more elaborate in the way of furniture

173

than a rough wooden bench and a heap of dry straw. There was a porcelain jug in one corner which looked almost exactly like pictures Ryker had seen of antique chamber pots, and which was apparently here for precisely the same purpose.

And the bars were . . . bars. It would have taken someone a lot stronger than he was to bend them out of their sockets.

After a while, he dozed off, awakening a time later when guards unlocked the door and entered his cell to bring him forth for judgment. The guards were a hardier lot than Thoh's retinue, too, like Captain Aoth. Ryker began to guess that his first impression of the Zhiamese was, after all, mistaken. Courtiers and nobles here in Zhiam were about as effete and elegant and dainty of person as courtiers and nobles are commonly supposed to be, he thought. But there were some decent men here in the City, just the same.

He was led out into the open, into a sort of courtyard. Strange glowing flowers shimmered against the dark, luminous and glossy; graceful feather trees spread their soft plumage to the night breeze, and fountains splashed somewhere in the darkness.

Here Ryker was told to step into a light wheeled vehicle for which he had no name. It was too small to be called a carriage, and too capacious to be considered a chariot. But when he saw the thing that was harnessed to draw the wheeled car, he promptly forgot all about the vehicle itself.

Was this the remote, prehistoric ancestor of the *slidar*? If so, it was improbably beautiful, like some fantastic creature in a fairy tale.

Imagine a six-legged animal all lean and sinewy and

graceful as a leopard, but five times as large, and covered with glittering enameled scales like a reptile, and you will have a faint idea of what it looked like. The creature had a long, gracefully arched neck somewhat like a fine horse, but longer. Also horselike, it was restive and spirited, pawing at the stone pave with delicate clawed feet. Its entire slim, beautifully proportioned body was a glittering tapestry of gold and green scales, like *cloisonné* or rare Oriental inlay work. And when it turned its slim, tapering head to peer back at Ryker, he gasped, for it had the long curved beak of an ibis or a crane, and immense, fathomless eyes like huge gems of dark purple, and a nodding crest of rosy filaments like some griffin or wyvern of fable.

The chariot, or whatever it was, got underway. Rapidly trotting along on its six astounding limbs, the gorgeous beaked reptilian creature glided swiftly out of the courtyard and into a broad boulevard lined with fantastic trees covered with huge blossoms like powder puffs, tinted pastel colors, pink and soft blue and a delicate shade of orange. Dawn was breaking overhead and the sky was a rich scarlet and vermilion and palest gold. The fairylike beauty of the scene made Ryker catch his breath.

At this early hour few were up, and the streets were empty under the blaze of morn. The beaked reptile bore the light chariot down a magnificent avenue lined with palaces or villas such as Ryker had only seen before moldering in decay, bitten deep by the teeth of time. But these were fresh and new and in excellent repair.

Then—and for the first time—did he truly realize in the depths of his heart that he had been transported by some weird, uncanny magic back into the ancient past of immemorial Mars. The sensation was a difficult one to convey. Something of what Ryker felt as he drove down that empty boulevard past splendid edifices of gleaming, fulvous marble in a vehicle drawn by some incredible beast of fable, you or I would feel, were we suddenly and miraculously transported to the Ishtar Gate of Babylon in the days when Nebuchadnezzar reigned, or that holy sacred city at the headwaters of the Nile which Akhnaten the Heretic Pharaoh had built to the glory of his god Aton, or gorgeous Persepolis before the mighty Macedonian conqueror put it to the torch.

And in that moment he knew that, no matter what Zarouk said or the gaunt fanatic, Dmu Dran, believed, these people were no worshippers of Evil and Old Night. Surely, deviltry and black sorcery could not flourish here, in surroundings so lovely, so impossibly gorgeous, that they took his breath away and left him numb and shaken with awe.

Whatever Zhagguaziu—the Fire Devil—actually was, if he was anything at all beyond a mere myth, the folk who worshipped him were not sinful fiends, but a graceful, courteous, beauty-loving people with an immensely advanced civilization and a culture rich with appreciation of the arts and of gracious living. *How, then, could the god they worshipped be a demon of evil?*

The answer was that he couldn't.


The hall in which Valarda received him was smaller than he might have expected, and incredibly beautiful.

The floor and walls were covered with glistening ceramic tiles, durable and gleaming as fine porcelain, and ornamented with geometrical arabesques quite unlike the ordinary native decorative arts. If they resembled anything in particular, it was the complex and intricate designs on Islamic tiles from the Middle Ages.

Carpets of sleek fur were scattered about the floor of the

large, high-ceilinged room. That they were the hides of hitherto unknown beasts was unquestionable, since fur-bearing mammals were all but extinct on the Mars he knew. Brick-red and carnation and dark bronze were the furs, and to tread upon their softness was like walking on clouds.

Despite the modest proportions of the room—for it was little more than an antechamber to the enormous pillared rotunda wherein Valarda generally held her court—quite a number of personages were crowded therein. This was the largest gathering of the Lost Nation that Ryker had ever seen close up, and he looked about him curiously. One and all were dressed in abbreviated garments which left plenty of naked flesh bare, the only exception to this fashion being old Melandron himself. The sage was robed in soft, clinging stuff which looked like velour.

Some of the younger nobles had the same soft, effete, underdeveloped look to them that he had observed in Lord Thoh's retinue when it had surprised him at the entrance to the underground road. But many of the older lords were heavier of build, with stronger character in their faces, and the look of competence and virility about them. The women, even the older women, were singularly beautiful.

Even in so lustrous a company, Valarda shone out like a diamond among pebbles. Her shimmering cataract of silken black hair was held in the same openwork coronal of gold filigree she had worn on the parapet. Her tawny limbs, svelte and nearly nude, flashed with priceless gems. Suspended between her shallow, firm breasts an immense, purple jewel blazed like a captive star. It was a rare ziriol, he knew, and its value was incalculable.

This time the face she turned to him was serene, resolute and untroubled. She was in control of her emotions, and the calm emotionlessness of her features, if they masked an inner turmoil of guilt or indecision, revealed no trace of this to the observing eye.

She sat on a low, carven bench of sparkling crystal, and, alone of that company, she was seated. Ryker had suspected her rank to be of the highest, and Thoh's term for her—"Priestess" it translated to—suggested as much. Now her supremacy among this company was obvious. And Ryker relaxed a little. It never hurts to have a friend on the throne.

Standing near Melandron, Ryker was surprised and relieved to see Herzog. The old scientist had been less seriously injured in his fall through the hidden trapdoor than Ryker had first feared, and from the lively expression on his face and the sprightly manner in which he held himself, he seemed to have made a full recovery.

"Ryker, my boy!" he sang out as the tall Earthling came into the chamber amidst his escort of guards. He wove his way through the throng and came over to grin happily up at the younger man.

"Hey, Doc, you're all in one piece, eh?" grinned Ryker. "That's good news! What's going on here, anyway?"

The old Israeli sobered. "Good news and bad news," he muttered. "We're to be judged, my boy, and it don't look good."

He nodded to where Lord Thoh stood, accoutered like a peacock in bejewelled finery that would have made Haroun Al-Raschid blush with envy. "That fellow over there is no friend of ours, let me tell you. Seems this place is split into two factions—politics, business as usual, even here!—and he leads the one that wants to go out and fight against our old friend, Zarouk, and his desert bandits, using the ancient weapons of science magic the ancestors of these people used long ago. Well, sir, the other faction, led by the Lady herself, thinks they better stick to the old laws against bloodshed—"

Ryker drew a breath. "So it *is* their law, then! I about had it figured that way, from the fact that the Stone Giants never took a life. Wonder if Zarouk knew about the law all the time? It sure would explain how he dared come into Zhiam with such a small force, when for all he knew he would be facing thousands of armed warriors."

"Yes," Doc nodded, "and the trouble is, see, Valarda—she's not only descended from the royal blood of these people, but the chief priestess of the Fire Devil—is holding her sway with quite a bit of difficulty, here. She's had to compromise, fact is. Had to give in to Thoh on this one point, just to hold her coalition together."

"What do you mean by that?" demanded Ryker.

Doc looked apologetic, as if he hated to be the bearer of bad news.

"Well . . . I mean we're already sentenced to death, both of us," he admitted. "The only question they have yet to decide is—*how.*"

## 22. Down There

THAT NIGHT IN HIS cell, Ryker had a visitor. It was about the last visitor he could have expected, considering the death sentence that had been passed against him and the old Israeli.

He was aroused from his fitful, uneasy slumbers by the clink of metal against metal, and the scrape of sandal leather against gritty stone.

Raising himself up on one elbow, he blinked through the gloom to see two robed and hooded figures at the door. The brilliant light from the crystal lamps which illuminated the corridor outlined their shadowy forms.

*"Ryker!"* whispered a faint voice. That voice he knew, and to hear again its husky music sent a quiver through his nerves which he could neither suppress nor deny. He got up quietly, so as not to disturb Doc, who lay snoring loudly against the wall, and padded over to the cell door on bare feet.

The taller of the two figures tossed back its hood, and it was Valarda.

"What d'you want?" he grunted. "After what you had to say back there, I figured there'd be nothing else to say—my Lady."

His voice was heavy with sarcasm, and she winced at the sound of it. Then she raised her face and looked into his eyes, and that which he saw written in her features, the suffering, the sorrow, made him wish he hadn't spoken so harshly.

"I want to try to make you understand," she whispered.

"Well, you can try," he said gruffly. "Go ahead."

Her face was wan and pale, and there were lines of strain and weariness about her glorious eyes. She stepped closer to the bars which stood between them—so close that he could smell the spicy scent of her unbound hair, and the warm perfume of her naked flesh.

"I hold my throne with difficulty here," she whispered. "To wield the power that is my inheritance from the ancient warrior princes of my blood, I must yield on some points. Can you understand that?"

He grinned humorlessly. "My death may be a small point to *you*, but it's mighty important to me! But go on, I'm listening."

Tears glittered in her thick lashes and her voice broke.

"Do you believe, Ryker, that your death is a small matter to me? Has there been naught between us that would suggest otherwise?"

His eyes fell and he grunted something she could not hear. Her eyes were fixed on his half-averted face, pleadingly.

"I have given you my lips, is that nothing? Do you believe that one of my lineage gives of herself lightly? I, who have never loved before—do you believe me to be incapable of love—even for a stranger from another world?"

Something rose within him then, within his heart. Something perilously near to . . . hope.

He looked at her somberly. "Love? We never spoke of it. You left me alone and among enemies, to die. Do you call that love?"

She nodded bravely. "Yes—love! The love of my people let me overrule the dictates of my heart, there on

181

the isthmus. But you did not die, Ryker. *Nor need you die now.*"

"Keep talking," he muttered.

"Listen closely, then. You will be given to the God tomorrow. You and the old man. You will descend into the Holy-of-Holies to stand before the Presence. Whether you live or die depends upon you—upon that which is in your heart. This much I have managed to wring from Lord Thoh and his followers—that we do not ourselves violate the ancient Vow our ancestors took before the God. It is the God alone who will be the cause of your death, if He so chooses!"

Ryker looked at her, thoughtfully. It was difficult to make out whether her god was real or whether she only believed him to be real. He knew so little about this Fire Devil the Lost Nation worshipped. There were so many questions, and so little time!

"We have a chance, then, to come through the ordeal alive?" he asked.

"Yes. Exactly that—a chance, nothing more. Others before you have gone down into the abyss, for one sin or another. Never were they seen alive again, for such was the Judgment of the God. But when you stand before Him, and He reads your heart, it is within His power to let you live. I pray with all of my own heart that it be so . . . oh, Ryker, Ryker . . . *why did you ever come into my life to trouble me?*"

She sagged against the bars, faint with weakness, and his strong arms went about her gently, and there, for the second time, he kissed her warm lips and felt the fragrance of her breath against his face.

"I have asked myself a thousand times how I could give my heart to a man of another race, another world, and I have found no answer for it," she breathed under his

182

kisses. "Save that you are strong and whole and clean, with a strength the men of my people no longer possess. Oh, Ryker!—my beloved!—when you stand before the God tomorrow—hold my image in your heart!"

"My Lady, it is time for the changing of the guard, and we must be gone," murmured the other robed figure. And only now did Ryker notice that it was Melandron. She nodded, and stepped back reluctantly from his embrace. Brushing the tears from her face she smiled at him, one small, brave smile.

Then they were gone.

Ryker went slowly back to his pallet and lay there, staring up at the roof of the cell.

Whether he lived or died tomorrow, he had won the love of the most beautiful woman of two worlds. Maybe that meant that dying for her was worthwhile, after all.


Beneath the Temple where Valarda reigned, a great stone stair wound down into the bowels of Mars. And by that mighty stair, Ryker and Herzog descended the following day.

With them went Valarda and Melandron and many others, among these the smiling Lord Thoh and even little Kiki, whom Ryker had not seen before during his brief visit to the City.

The faces of those who escorted the two Earthlings were solemn and they wore the shadow of fear. There was little conversation between the lords. For the most part, they maintained a hushed and reverent silence. Ryker got the feeling that they would all be glad to leave this immense, cavernous space where dwelt eternally the strange and awesome divinity they worshipped.

Only Lord Thoh seemed jubilant and merry.

Ryker himself felt nothing at all. There was nothing in

this Abyss, he knew, for he had long ago given up childish beliefs in gods and devils. He had an inkling of what he was about to face, and when they reached at length the bottom of the stair, he grinned bleakly to find his guess correct.

A vast open space lay hidden here far below the crust of Mars, the arched roof far overhead supported by columns of massive stone, like the pillars of some tremendous cathedral.

Roof and walls and columns were alike encrusted with some glittering crystalline deposit. A dim, sourceless phosphorescence glimmered here in the depths, and this pale, wan luminescence was reflected in the glassy stuff of the mineral encrustation as from a million mirrors, until all of the vast and shadowy emptiness was made ghostly with wandering lights. Like will-o'-the-wisps, vague centers of radiance drifted to and fro between the huge columns, and twinkled in the facets of dangling stalactites, as in the glassy pendants of so many crystal chandeliers.

The floor of the vast, echoing cavern was smooth and regular, no doubt so shaped by the toil of men.

He looked around, admiring the fantastic scene. But there was nothing here to feel afraid of, for nothing lived in this Aladdin's cave of glittering crystal and twinkling lights.

In the center of the floor was a vast pit whose sides were unnaturally smooth and regular and whose shaft went down to an unguessable depth.

Before this pit three stone spears had been left standing by the workmen who had cleared the cavern floor down to the primal bedrock. Fastened to these stalagmites were bronze shackles and chains.

They had been there a very long time, for they were old and deeply bitten by the teeth of time, green and scaly with verdigris.

Within them hung three skeletons—grisly, gaunt things of dead bone, staring at the pit with sightless, gaping sockets, grinning with mirthless, bony jaws.

These the guards unlocked from their chains, and cast them clattering away.

They chained Ryker and Herzog to the stony spears.

The spears rose from the cavern's floor on the very brink of the enormous, circular pit. The two Earthlings were bound in such a way that they must face that yawning pit forever . . . until death came to claim then . . . or the God to judge them.

Only two they were, and the third stalagmite remained untenanted, its chains hanging loose and empty. Ryker grinned. It was like him to grin in the face of death, and a bit of gallows humor couldn't hurt.

*There were three thieves at Golgotha,* he thought to himself with grim irreverence. *Of course, one of them was no thief. . . .*

The shackles were locked, and it was all over but the dying. That would be a slow, tedious business, but thirst and hunger would do the trick in time. There would be a lot of time, thought Ryker. All the time in the world.

He wondered vaguely how long their bones would hang in these chains, until tossed aside to make room for the next condemned men. Not that it mattered much.

The Martians are much given to ritual, but in this case there was none at all. Once they had seen the two men chained to the stone spears on the brink of the pit, they turned about and went back by the way they had come. It was as if they were, all of them, anxious to leave this dreadful place of wandering lights and faint echoes and crawling shadows.

Valarda looked one last time into Ryker's grim, glowering eyes. Her face was pale and pinched, her warm lips

185

colorless, but hope glowed in her eyes. Then she dropped thick lashes to hide the naked candor of her gaze, and vanished from Ryker's line of sight.

The others filed past, some glancing at him curiously, others averting their eyes as if ashamed of what had been done here.

Thoh gave his victim one bright glance of cold mockery, and an ironic wave of his hand as if to say goodbye, before he, too, began to ascend the stair.

Ryker and Doc stood there in the chains for a long time without speaking, until the last far, faint echo of shuffling feet died into silence far above them.

And they were left alone with only their thoughts to keep them company.

And shadows, and echoes, and vague, wandering lights.

*Forever* . . .

Forever is a long time. And here there was no way of measuring time.

After a while their arms and the muscles of back and shoulders began to ache from the strain of the awkward position in which the two men were chained.

After a while the torment ebbed, as if flesh had endured all it could, and numbness crept in, dulling the agony.

After a time the numbness, too, faded, and they could feel nothing at all in their arms. It was as if they were being slowly turned into men of stone, like the faceless Giants who had warded and watched the walls of Zhiam.

Thirst, too, became a torment. But hours—or days— later, they became unaware of thirst.

They were bound in too uncomfortable a position to be able to sleep. Every time their consciousness faded, and they sagged forward in the chains, the sharp bite of the scale bronze shackles knifing into the flesh of their wrists roused them.

They found their minds wandering. Ryker thought of soft beds and cool gardens and dewy goblets of wine and splashing fountains for a while. Then his mind seemed to drift away into waking dreams. Faces rose into his memory that he had long forgotten, the faces of friends and of foes. For a time he played in the summery garden of that white frame house, in the shadows of tall trees, with the small black and white dog. Even that dream faded and fled away at length, and his mind became blank and gray and empty. . . .

Suddenly a faint sound broke the trance that gripped Ryker's dreaming mind. Something broke his vague reverie.

He turned his head to the right, ignoring the sting of pain in stiff muscles. Doc hung in the chains, his face pale and empty, his head sagging upon his bony breast, silvery wisps of hair disordered. He was unconscious, or dead. Either way, it was better so.

But the sound which had disturbed Ryker had not come from that source.

There it was again! A faint scuffle, the clatter of stone against stone.

From *behind* him . . .

And sweat came popping out all over Ryker's nearly-naked body, as a thought of pure horror crashed into his numb brain.

*What if there were rats down here?*

From dim, half-conscious dreaming, he came suddenly, terribly awake. Fully conscious now, his mind ablaze with merciless clarity, he remembered that the subterranean caverns of the Southlands were tunneled and teeming with the huge carnivorous rodents the Martians hunted for *orthavva* furs . . . rats the size of small dogs, they were, he knew.

And the blood congealed in his veins as the sheer, hopeless horror of his predicament burst upon his mind in all its implications.

Surely, in all the annals of human experience, there was no more ghastly way of dying than being devoured alive by rats.

That faint scuffle sounded again behind him.

*Then something touched the back of his leg and Ryker almost fainted.*

In the next split-second he nearly fainted again, but this time from a different emotion. For he felt like one snatched from the burning floor of Hell and set down amidst the gardens of Paradise.

For, just behind him, Kiki said, "*Do you yet live, man?*"

## 23. The Sacrifice

THE BOY WAS weary and bedraggled and travel stained, and he had been weeping, for tearstains were visible beneath his green eyes where they had cut through the coating of dust.

He was entirely naked, gray with dust from head to foot, with a smudge on his cheek, or possibly a bruise. His feet were dirty with stains of crushed mold or lichen, and rough, sharp stones had cut those little feet until they bled.

He left wet red marks on the stone floor as he limped to where Ryker hung in the chains.

Ryker stared down at the dusty, bedraggled lad, eyes wide with unbelief and filled with the dawning of hope. He had never been fond of the mischievous imp. Now he felt that he had never been so glad to see anyone in his entire life.

The boy wound his arms around Ryker's waist and buried his dusty head against Ryker, and made strange, hoarse, coughing sounds. At first he could not identify these noises. Then it came to him that the boy was trying to sob, but that his throat was dry with dust, as dry as Ryker's own.

"Kiki . . . why are you here?" he croaked through dry lips. The boy lifted his head to peer into Ryker's face with eyes wild, yet curiously dull.

"They have come into the City," he said tonelessly. "The Outlanders. My Lady has fallen from power. Prince

189

Thoh leads the men, now, and he has condemned My Lady to face the God.''

"*Prince* Thoh it is now, is it?'' rasped the big man heavily, twitching his cracked lips into a ghastly caricature of a smile.

Then the meaning of Kiki's words hit him, and he stiffened.

*They meant to hang Valarda in the chains on the third stone spear.*

They meant her to die the slow, awful death to which he and Doc were condemned.

Ryker growled, deep in his chest, like an animal. Through the dusty tangle of his disordered locks, his eyes glared like the eyes of a lion. Suddenly, weariness and stiffness and pain left him. He felt filled with a terrible strength, a strength of fury and desperation.

"The chains, boy,'' he gasped. "Get them off me . . . break them, cut them . . . *get me loose!*''

After a time, Kiki gave up the futile attempt to free Ryker from his chains, and collapsed in a sobbing heap at the feet of the Earthling.

Even though corrosion had eaten deeply into the hard bronze of the shackles, neither Ryker's strength nor Kiki's cunning and agile fingers could free the tall man of his bonds.

The Earthling looked down at the boy huddled at his feet, his hard face gentle.

"It's all right, Kiki. Don't cry. You did the best you could.''

"It wasn't good enough,'' the boy said in a choked voice.

"Maybe not. But you did the very best you could, and that's all anybody can do—their best.''

Doc, who had recovered consciousness during the past half an hour, and who had watched the boy's labor with sympathetic eyes, uttering encouraging noises from time to time, now lifted his head and stared up. Distant echoes sounded above them, coming from the shaft over their heads, and the stair. The echoes of footsteps descending.

"They're coming already," the old man observed.

"I guess so," muttered Ryker somberly. "You go hide yourself now, Kiki. No, not back there—among those stalagmites on the opposite side of the pit. Hurry, now, before they see you."

The boy scampered off, and Ryker and the Israeli were alone again. But not for very long.

The party that entered the cavern was largely the same as had brought Ryker and Doc Herzog to be chained to the stone spears. Missing were a few of Valarda's supporters; present were very many more of Thoh's faction.

Thoh himself now walked proudly, features molded in an expression of haughty disdain. Only the eager, febrile glitter in his eyes revealed how deliciously Lord Thoh— Prince Thoh—revelled in his newly acquired power. It was obviously the culmination of a dream he had long nurtured in secret.

And now it was Valarda's turn to play the humble captive, bound and helpless, soon to face the judgment of her god. The Priestess held her head high, and her expression was proud and unafraid, but she was pale as death and the shadow of dread haunted her golden eyes.

The guards were uneasy and looked harried and crestfallen. Their captin, a man called Hartha, no longer led them. Apparently, he had remained loyal to his Priestess, or Prince Thoh considered him likely to prove disloyal to the new regime. Taking his place at the head of the guards was a grinning rascal named Sastro whom

191

Ryker remembered having seen in Thoh's retinue on an earlier occasion.

Valarda had been stripped of her plumed coronal and most of her gems, but she did not seem to have been used by rough hands nor offered any indignities, insofar as was apparent from her appearance or demeanor.

They chained her to the third spear, tugging the chains taut so that her arms were forced above her head. She endured this without a word of complaint, without permitting a sound to escape her lips. Ryker growled and glowered. If looks could kill, the smirking prince would have been struck dead on the spot.

"We have brought you some feminine companionship to lighten the boredom of your wait, Outworlder," Thoh smiled. He was well aware of Ryker's smoldering rage, and it amused him. A chained lion, however ferocious, can be safely taunted. And Ryker was still chained.

"You may face the judgment of your god before we do," remarked the old Israeli with tranquil relish. The prince glanced at him, surprised. Doc Herzog grinned, and added, "The enemy is at your gates, already. Or maybe even inside the City by this time. Your reign is likely to be a short one, so enjoy it while it lasts!"

Thoh paled to the lips at this impertinence from so unexpected a source, and half raised his hand as if to strike the old man in the face. Then he thought better of it, and turned a glance of pure venom upon the proud, silent figure of Valarda.

"It was this witch's doing," he snarled. And his features, distorted by the intensity of his rage, lost for a moment their smooth, effeminate prettiness, and became vicious. "If she had given me the men I wanted, and let me ride forth against the invaders, to use against them the

192

weaponry our ancestors used once, long ago, against *their* ancestors—''

''Probably wouldn't have done you much good,'' growled Ryker. ''Your folks lost that war too, I understand.''

Thoh looked him up and down, his face cold and heavy. Then he spat deliberately between Ryker's feet. Ryker looked him straight in the eye and grinned. There was no humor in it but a baring of white teeth, as a wolf grins before it bites. Thoh took an involuntary step backwards, then bit his lip, hating himself for momentarily letting his weakness show.

He stepped forward and struck Ryker across the face— once—twice—three times—slapping Ryker's head back against the stone of the spear to which he was chained. Ryker held the grin steady, although a trickle of red blood ran down his chin from a cut on his mouth. Thoh flushed and stepped back, panting.

''The God will judge us all,'' remarked Valarda in a serene, untroubled voice. ''Those who kept the Vow and those who would break it.''

''The god you worship sleeps,'' said Thoh shortly. ''Not since the time of our grandsires has He awakened from His slumbers. You may expect little help from *that* quarter, My Lady! No . . . here you will remain while the world grows old . . . you will hang in those chains until your tongue  swells with thirst and your belly shrinks with hunger, and you go mad and die raving . . . raving to a god who cannot even hear you, and who will never wake again.''

At that moment there was an interruption.

One of the lords who stood near Thoh uttered an exclamation, pointing beyond them, across the pit.

Thoh turned, and all eyes looked in that direction. Ryker, too, looked—then froze with horror.

Upon the far side of the pit a small, slight figure came into view. A young lad, naked and dust-stained and desperate. He stood upon the very brink of the pit, staring down to unguessable depths. The expression on his face was terrible to see.

"Kiki! Don't!" Ryker yelled hoarsely. The boy did not even raise his head to look in his direction.

"I must," he panted. "I must do the very best I can."

Valarda stared at him, unbelieving. Her lips parted, and she strove to speak, but fear had paralyzed her tongue and she could utter no sound.

"Why, it is the little imp," muttered Thoh distractedly. "However did he get here—and what is he about?"

"He's going to jump!" said Sastro. Thoh looked at him questioningly.

"Whatever for?"

Then Kiki raised his thin arms above his tousled head and cried out—

"For my Lady! For her! O, God of my people—*awaken!*"

And hurled himself over the brink, and fell.

Ryker shut his eyes, feeling sick. Valarda choked back a sob and let her head fall forward so that her long hair hid her face. And the old Israeli said something in a low voice. It was in Hebrew and none of them could understand that tongue, but it sounded like a prayer.

The others looked at one another. Thoh seemed curiously effected. He bit his lip, eyes hooded, brooding upon the pit where the young boy had fallen to his death. His expression was unreadable.

*And then there came another interruption.*

From the shadows, Zarouk strode forth, grinning, a

long sword naked in his hand. Behind him others moved, muttering, their hands heavy with steel. It would seem that the invaders had followed Prince Thoh and his retinue, descending the great stair in silence, careful to conceal their presence.

Zarouk looked at Thoh, then at Ryker and Valarda. He grinned hugely and waved his sword in a mocking salute. His desert raiders crowded close behind him, eyeing Thoh's guards belligerently, eager for the kill.

One rush, and victory would be theirs. And they knew it.

The next surprise, however, was that of Thoh. For he shrugged back his heavy cloak, and showed the desert men his hands. They were tender and soft, those hands, and there were too many jeweled rings upon their fingers, but now they bore something else.

Ryker's guns. The guns that Valarda had stolen from him when he had slept his drugged sleep, there on the isthmus when she had deserted him.

Ryker had forgotten all about them. He knew they must be somewhere here in Zhiam, but he had not thought about them.

Evidently, Prince Thoh had.

His slim, beringed hands might be soft and womanish, but they bore a heavy weight of death.

And now it was Thoh's turn to smile and Zarouk who paled, bit his lip, looked uncertain, and stepped backwards, lowering his sword.

A deadly tension grew in the air between the two groups of men. Taut it was and near to breaking. And when it broke, guns would rave and steel would flash crimson and blood would be spilt—here, in this holy place, even here!

*And then, the last interruption—*

From far away, the murmur of bells. Many they were,

195

faint and far—a distant chiming, cold and pure and sweet! Like bells of glass or crystal . . . like tiny chimes of ice . . . ringing, crystalline music!

And, from the dark mouth of the pit wherein Kiki had thrown himself, a faint glimmer of dim light—cold it was, and blue and white, like brilliance that was reflected from mirrors of ice.

The music rang clearer now, and sharper!

The dim luminescence about the mouth of the pit . . . brightened!

Whatever it was, it was coming up the shaft—*and getting nearer!*

## 24. Child of Stars

LIGHT—PURE, SPARKLING LIGHT—poured up out of the black pit like a fountain of shimmering fire!

The cold and awful glory of it shone back from thrice ten thousand crystal facets, till every plane and angle of the cavern, every mineral encrustation, every glassy stalactite, blazed like a billion, billion diamonds, reflecting an utterness of light, a purity of light, beyond description as it was beyond belief.

One of the bandits sank to the cavern floor in a crouch, huddling in the dust. He covered glazed, horror-struck eyes with hands that shook, shielding his gaze from that ineffable radiance.

"*Zhagguaziu* . . ." he moaned. Then said no more; neither did he move.

Zarouk stared into the seething splendor, his face blank with awe. Forgotten now were his red dreams of conquest and empire. He looked upon the glorious god he had thought to be a demon, and there was wonder in his heart, childlike and simple.

The blaze of glory faded now, as if the splendid creature somehow realized that its brilliance was too intolerable for mortal men to bear. It . . . *veiled* itself, and dimmed its fires a bit, and floated there in midair above the floor of the cavern.

Ryker blinked through tear filled eyes, trying to make out its shape and nature through the blinding light. There

197

was an inner core of brilliance brighter than the rest, a slim, tapering spindle, like the flame that dances on the wick of a candle. This was light of an utter purity of white, a spark of white—one spark, perchance, of that supernal flame that burns in the heart of stars.

But between the awful glory of that inner core, lacy veils of shimmering luminescence, filmy and fragile—like the wings of moths, shimmering and shot through with a thousand tints and hues—like floating draperies of sheerest gauze, spun by sorcery from the stuff of glowing opals—drifted and swirled and coiled about the brilliance of the core, veiling it from view.

Whatever it was, it was no devil. It was too beautiful to exist, too lovely to be real. And far too perfect in its glory to have aught of evil within it.

Pure light it was, pure energy, like the soul of a star.

Somehow—although it had no eyes, no organs of any kind—it saw them, the puny creatures of flesh and bone and blood that crouched or huddled or cowered far beneath its airy dance.

And somehow, although it had no mouth, no organs of speech, it spoke to them. The voice of the Glory was a thin, cold song and it whispered deep within their very minds, that song, cold and sweet and wild as the polar winds that sang through pinnacles of ice at the utter and secret pole of the world.

*Why dost thou feed life to me, when sacrifice is forbidden from of old, and I have no need of such sustenance?*

Sweet, sweet was the singing of the Glory within their brain, cool, and serene, and passionless.

*It was such a little life, so short, so young! Thou knowest that I have forbidden the taking of life, and will not countenance the shedding of blood. Poor, puny crea-*

*tures that ye be, with lives as brief as any candle-flame, why must ye shorten that which is already cruelly brief? Thy offering I return to thee, and I must chastise thee, and sternly, that ye sin in this manner against me no more.*

Veils of drifting coruscation drew aside, parted asunder . . . and there, cradled and swathed in living light was the boy, Kiki, naked and beautiful and alive, his face gentle and dreaming, his eyes filled with wonder.

"Kiki!" breathed Valarda, breathlessly. The swirling mists of brilliance deposited the boy, whole and unharmed, upon the cavern floor. He stretched bare arms, and yawned, showing a little pink tongue, then looked about him dazedly, as bemused as one who just awakened from strange and lovely dreams.

Seeing Valarda and Ryker and Herzog chained to the stony stalagmites, he smiled and came over to them. About his body there yet clung a dim, pulsing luminescence, a wisp of that greater Glory which filled all of the cavern with its splendor.

He touched their chains with shining fingers and, somehow, strangely, they were free.

First he freed Valarda in this manner, then the old Israeli, and Ryker last of all. Pausing before Ryker, he looked up into the man's dark face, wonderingly.

"Oh!" he murmured. "You are weary, and you thirst! But that should not be. A moment—*there!*"

He touched Ryker with glowing hands—brow, mouth and breast—and gently, as a child might touch an injured dove. A weird, cold thrill ran through Ryker's nerves, an icy tingle, electric yet bracing. And then he felt the weakness and stiffness and the exhaustion drain from his lame and weary muscles and numb limbs. It drained away and it was gone, as if it had never been. He flexed strong hands,

199

unbelievingly. Even the sores on his wrists, where scaly verdigris-eaten metal had bitten deep in his flesh as he fought the shackles, even those were healed. And so was the thirst that tortured him, and he felt whole and well and filled with strength again, like one who wakens from a deep, long sleep, refreshed and invigorated.

The boy turned to look at the hovering Glory.

"Did I do it right, Lord?" he inquired.

*Thou knowest that it is well done,* said the Glory. *And now touch thou the old one, too, and heal his suffering.*

The boy smiled dreamily and went to where the old scientist hung in his chains, his lined and homely face filled with awe and wonderment. The boy said something to the old man shyly, and touched him with light-misted fingers as he had touched Ryker.

"What . . . have you done . . . to Kiki, Lord?" whispered Valarda.

*Ah, my priestess!* laughed the Glory, chiming with faint music as it swirled about to regard her. *She who would have kept the Vow, and lost her throne for keeping it! The child, you ask? He hath only died. His poor, broken flesh it is within my power to heal, but to make him live again—aiee!—am I a god, that I can restore life to the dead? Nay! But a tiny portion of myself I placed within his breast, that he might live again—changed, is he, and yet the same child that ye knew. Only, a little different.*

Ryker went over to where Valarda knelt before the Glory, and raised her to her feet, and held her against his chest. Then he lifted his head and stared into the lacy, swirling mists of spangled light that veiled from their dazed eyes the splendors of the central fire.

"If you are not a god, what are you, then?" he asked through stiff lips.

The veils of moted splendor swirled and coiled about the curdled purity of flame. A storm of tinkling chimes rang out and faded.

*I? I am—Life! Life without end and without beginning! Old as the stars am I, who once was one with them . . . but that was long ago, O very long ago . . . at the Creation.*

The spangled mists writhed, floating vapors spun from pure light drifting on the air their opal luminescence. The blazing spindle at the core seemed to fade, then to brighten, then to ebb again, like the slow pulsing of a mighty heart.

*When the Universe began was I born . . . one with the stars was I, but different—different! For I lived, and knew that I lived, and the great suns about me knew not that they lived . . . thus was I alone in my sentience and my being, and they, the stars, of which I had been born, they knew me not, nor danced as I danced in my joy, for I alone lived.*

"Child-of-Stars," whispered Doc Herzog faintly, staring up into the Glory. "Born of the chance interplay of energy—perhaps once in a billion times a billion years such a thing is born, a creature of pure energy, self-sustaining, eternal—"

The Glory laughed, like silver bugles ringing faint and far.

*"Yes, the Child-of-Stars am I! Long ages did I drift through the starry spaces, seeking to find another such as I to be my friend. But there was no other one such as I, for I was alone in all that vast immensity! And so, in time, I came down to this little world, as I had visited ten thousand others in my quest, and here—here I found living things that knew and felt and loved and thought, even as I. Different from the Child-of-Stars they were,*

201

*their core of splendor trapped in a prison-house of flesh, but, yet, more like to me than aught that I had found among the cold and empty splendor of the star-thronged galaxies. So here I dwelt, befriending the little creatures, one tribe of them that did not flee from me in terror . . . ah, it was long and long ago!"*

"A billion years, maybe," breathed Herzog.

*So long as that? Mayhap, old man. But when their brothers turned to rend them for that they worshipped me, I brought them here, here to Zhiam, here to the City that we built together outside the world. Ah, it was hard, hard to open wide the Doors of Time to bring them here to Yesterday, but I was young and strong and filled with love for them, my friends, my people, my little brethren, and I worked the wonder! So that they should be safe from the enmity and the hatred of their own kind, I brought them here to this place and to this age which even time itself had forgotten, and which no men knew, for here it is a billion years before the first men rose to sentience upon this planet, and here I gave unto them that land of peace and plenty, even as I had sworn that I would do . . . if they would only keep sacrosanct that Vow which I extracted from them, that no life should be taken here, and no blood spilt.*

Doc's old face, lifted to the Glory, was saintly, enthralled, rapt with fascination as he drank in this uncanny tale of a vast exodus across the ages. And, perhaps, he was remembering another age, and another exodus, and another people whose God had brought them also out of bondage and peril, into a promised land of peace and plenty that was to be theirs, so long as they held true to another Vow, and obeyed another set of Commandments.

*But that was long and long ago, I see . . . and there be those among my children who weary of their obedience to that Vow, and would break it, and shed blood against my will . . . and others, too, sprung from the loins of ancient enemies, who have at length pursued us here across the ages! And who would now renew that old, forgotten war—ah, children! Children! How jealously you cling to those little toys of steel and iron that ye love so well—and to those newer toys, as I observe, which your brothers on a younger world nearer to the sun have brought hither . . . well, and well! Then I must chastise thee, and close the Door which ye have opened—and then? And then, ah, then—I shall sleep again, for as I slumbered long centuries here in this place below the world, what lovely dreams I knew, what lovely dreams! But, now, to my toil!*

And veils of lacy incandescence swirled wide like the bright wings of angels from Paradise, and swept them up, one and all—and the rocky cavern roof above their heads split asunder—and they rose, webbed about in scintillant splendor, and soared up above the City where bands of men fought and slew, and beasts screamed, and buildings burned with red flame, and black smoke dirtied the pure and lambent skies of morning.

Up to a towering height the Glory soared, and there, atop the great parapet that enclosed the utmost tier of the Temple, which was itself built upon the greatest height of the City, it left them, and they turned, dazed and dazzled, blinking in wonder at each other, and at themselves.

Valarda still clung to Ryker, and his arm was strong about her slim waist. They were beyond wonder now, and beyond awe and marvel, clinging together like children, seeking comfort in the warmth of sheltering arms and the nearness of another.

And they turned and looked down upon the City.

And the Glory fell upon the City, in a storm of crystalline chiming.

*So ye would war, would ye?* it sang—cold and serene and merciless was that piercing music! *Well, I shall teach you—war!*

## 25. When Gods War

ZHAIM LAY HELPLESS in the grip of the enemies who had come out of the deeps of time to slay and thieve and ravage.

Few indeed were the desert raiders Zarouk had brought with him, but even a few fighting men can cut a red swath through men with empty hands, who may not make or bear arms.

Such little as men may do to defend their wives and homes and children, the men of Zhiam had already done. Barricades had been built, streets blocked, doors locked, and women hidden away. But barricades may be torn down by many strong, determined hands, locked doors be beaten in, and houses burned. And when men with empty hands strive to shield their loved ones with their own bodies, sharp steel can rend asunder that flimsy barricade as well.

And Zarouk's horde was very good at its work.

Flames flickered in the ruins of gutted houses. Villas lay open, ravished of their lovely loot by swaggering conquerers. Men had been cut down and lay now staring with dead, uncomprehending eyes upon the ruin, from pools of spreading redness.

Women—especially those who were young and beautiful—were not slain. But there were those among them who ere long would wish for the benison of the knife, rather than the shame of serving their conquerors in the immemorial way in which the women of the conquered must serve their conquerors.

Palaces stood open, doors battered in, flames flickering through shattered windows, while rough, cursing men carried heaps of plunder through trampled gardens.

Children—those young enough, and desirable enough to make good slaves—huddled together, tongueless, wide eyed, under guard.

*Then, suddenly, the Glory was there.*

It was vaster now than it had been in the depths of the world, like some enormous cloud of scintillation and jewelled splendor, it hung above the rubble choked streets bestrewn with corpses, loot and nubile captives.

The desert hawks stared up at it curiously, wonderingly, then shrugged, and turned back to their red work.

There were many marvels in this strange world, and all were harmless. What is one marvel more?

They would learn soon enough, and to their sorrow.


Prone in a puddle of congealing gore, a dead man sprawled. He had been a guard stationed before the Temple, more a position of honor than aught else, in this paradisical world where there were no thieves or murderers, and his weapons were ornamental, little more. But his heart had been brave and true, and when the desert men came swaggering and laughing through the streets, he had gone against them, using only his bare hands and not the flimsy weapons at his side. And they had cut him down, slashing open his belly with a careless, backhand stroke, so that his bowels fell out upon the pavement.

He had fallen, then, still striving to protect that which he was here to ward. Fallen and died there on the cobbles, while rough men laughed and jeered and mocked him in his dying.

That had been almost an hour ago.

*But now . . . he lived.*

Jerkily—slowly—awkwardly, like a jointed puppet—the dead man got to his feet. And stood, spread legged, turning his head stiffly from side to side. His face was pale and dirty, and blood was upon it. His eyes were dull and filmed and his mouth hung slackly open.

The raiders nearest to him were piling gorgeous furnishings into a tottery heap. Fussing about them was Houm, fat, greedy Houm, his greasy lips smiling, his quick, clever eyes counting the value of the silken tapestries, the hand-carved ivory furniture, the jewel-studded vases, the precious things of jade and cinnabar and lapis.

Suddenly the smile went crooked on Houm's fat face.

For, stalking stiffly towards him, the dead man came.

He paled then, did Houm, and plucked at trembling lips with beringed fingers, babbling crazy things. For the walking corpse, with its belly slashed open and wet bowels dragging, went over to the first man and tore his throat out with cold, stiff hands.

The second man died just as quickly, for the corpse broke his neck. The third man backed off, swearing, cutlass-shaped sword out. Hoarsely, he commanded the slayer of his two comrades to halt, and when he would not halt the raider took a cut at him. The sword made red ruin of the dead man's face, but did not even slow him.

He twisted the raider's head off, and tossed it aside. The grisly thing rolled across the pavement to thump into the head of a plunderer.

Houm followed it with vacant eyes. He giggled.

But not for long.

The walking corpse, now faceless, was upon Houm then. He picked the fat man up as if he weighed no more than a doll, and broke his back across a bended knee, as a man might break a rotten stick.

So perished Houm, the merchant who had dreamt of the plunder of an entire world, and who now would inherit only six feet of it, or as much as makes a grave.

*And the Glory—laughed!*

Xinga was at the wall. He had been supervising the destruction of the Stone Giants, but now his work was done and the last of the enchanted colossi had been rendered helpless with nets or lassoes, and reduced to gravel under pounding war-hammers, mauls and axes.

Now, Xinga wanted some of the fun the other raiders had been enjoying.

He had found a girl and had taken her away from the warrior and was admiring his bit of plunder. She was a child of perhaps thirteen, slim and exquisite, with silken hair and faery eyes like wet jewels. A bit young for his tastes, to be sure, but hip and breast and thigh were firm and round with the promise of the woman she would one day become.

She begged him with pleading, eloquent eyes, for he had bound her lips with a gag; he laughed, telling her to relax and perhaps she would enjoy it, too. Then he stripped her rags from her and lay her on the trampled ground of her father's garden.

Ignoring her weak struggling, and the moans and whimpers which escaped from her gagged mouth, he lay down upon her and played with her bare breasts for a time, prolonging the moment when he would take her, finding the delay teasingly delicious.

Tossed into a gory heap near a broken alabaster fountain, her father and her brothers lay, hacked to red ruin. Now, as Xinga played with the girl, fondled and smiled as she writhed under the touch of his dirty fingers, he was too preoccupied to notice when the pile of corpses came apart and the dead boys and their father came stiffly to their feet and stalked over to where he lay amusing himself.

One took him by the leg, another by the arm, and the third by the head. They tore him apart.

Dmu Dran had remained behind to oversee the desecration of the Inner Shrine of the Temple. The little gaunt fanatic knew that his master, Zarouk, and a party of warriors had descended into the depths beneath the building in pursuit of the so-called Prince who had seized power, but it mattered little to him.

He was a priest, and must be about his holy business.

He had built a bonfire of the Zhiamese scrolls and sacred scriptures—beautiful painted parchments, covered with writing unknown to him, which had preserved from the lapse of time the ancient wisdom and philosophy and speculations of the sages.

They burned beautifully, he thought.

He had dragged from the heap of bound captives, taken when the Temple was first broken into, a young priest or novice. He was a boy, sixteen or seventeen at the most, and his eyes were wide and frightened, and he was praying to his god in a half-heard whisper.

Dmu Dran had cut his robes away, so that he would watch that adolescent nakedness writhe and wriggle in the flames.

When he had stripped the boy stark naked, he dragged him by the feet across the floor, then rolled him over on his belly into the fire.

The boy had screamed. But now, blackened and shrivelled, he was beyond screaming.

Dmu Dran was bending over the heap of captives, picking another victim for his holy work, when something took place behind him that he did not notice until the sound of scraping feet made him turn and . . . freeze.

The burnt boy had gotten up from his bed of fire and was dragging himself on stiff, black, withered legs towards his tormentor.

His face had been seared away to the naked bone of his skull, which was brown and greasy and still smoking.

Dmu Dran stared and stared, and then his eyes rolled up into his head until only the whites showed.

The burnt boy-priest took him by the back of the neck in a grip as strong as stone, and dragged him over to the bonfire where the precious scriptures smoldered, and thrust him face down into the coals, and held him there until he died.

The coals were hot and red and glowing, but it took him all of twenty minutes to die.


One by one the fires went out, for the Glory called the clouds and commanded them to rain.

There was by that time an army of corpses, and they stalked stiffly about, clearing away the rubble. Most of the raiders were dead by this time, and, after a while, they too, had risen and walked, and now toiled beside their victims, clearing away the wreckage and smothering the last few stubborn fires, and removing the ruins from where the gates of the City had been.

Not everyone in the City had been slain, of course. Some of the men lived, and almost all of the women and children, save those who had been taken by many men and had died therefrom.

Nor had all the raiders perished. Some few, quicker of thought than their brethren, had thrown down their swords and surrendered. These now huddled together without speaking, guarded by animated horrors that had once been dead. Some of the captives wept, or cursed in ragged, breathless monotones. But most of them just sat there with dead faces and empty eyes, waiting for doom, and glancing up from time to time at the Glory which drifted here and there above the towers.

There were many of the men and boys of the City who had been injured or maimed but were not yet dead. These were brought before Kiki and he healed them, one by one, with a touch of his hands whereon the supernal light yet lingered.

There were old men and women who had looked on too much horror, and women and children who had endured too much. These, whose minds had broken under their torment, were healed by Kiki too. Serene, forgetting that which they had endured, they smiled now, seeking out their friends and families among the living.

*After the slaying, you see, there is a time for healing,* the Glory observed in its cool, singing voice. *Is it not well, Lord Thoh?*

In a hushed voice, his face as pale and dead as one of the walking corpses, Lord Thoh agreed that it was well.

*You wanted war, did you not? For honor and glory and to prove your virility. Well, you have seen now, Lord Thoh, the red face of war. Did you find it . . . pretty?*

Thoh swallowed with a dry, aching throat. He had been sick five times during the scenes of carnage, and he had emptied his guts until there was nothing left to vomit up. Now, shakily, he said that war was . . . not pretty.

Zarouk maintained a cold, impassive mien. He had, however, closed his teeth upon his bottom lip to keep from

211

crying out while being forced to look on as his men were butchered by the walking dead they had slain.

He had bitten entirely through his lip, and the blood bedewed his beard and stained the front of his robe.

But he had not cried out.

*And you, Prince Zarouk? How do you like your conquest—and your empire? Shall I command the dead to build you a kingdom, whereover you may rule the dead men, and be served by them, forever?* the Glory inquired, sweetly.

No flicker of expression showed in the stony eyes of the Desert Hawk. "You are the victor here," he mumbled through maimed lips. "Do with me what you will."

*I shall, indeed!* laughed the Glory. *For in every contest, there is the victor and the vanquished. Shall I do with you, O Zarouk, as you would have done with the vanquished, had you been the victor here?*

Zarouk said nothing, but no longer did he hold his head so high. He was a beaten man.

And when it was all finished, and the City was cleared for rebuilding, and the injured healed and restored to their loved ones, there came a time for ending.

The Glory directed the army of the walking dead to leave Zhiam. They marched out into the great blue valley and dwindled from sight into the distance. Far, far from the City the unnatural vitality which sustained the illusion of life within them would withdraw, and they would find lonely graves in the wilderness, there to sleep forever.

*Now this is my decree,* said the Glory. *The victors shall dwell here with the vanquished, and together they shall toil to rebuild the City. Shoulder to shoulder they shall labor together, and perchance they shall in time discover*

212

*they are no different, one from the other, for all men are as brothers, although they forget this simple truth and let vain words and bits of painted cloth called flags and other futile, flimsy, frivolous things divide them, one from the other.*

*And, once again, I say unto you: abide by the Vow! Shed not the blood of beasts or men, nor slay aught that liveth, but dwell in peace and harmony with all life. Do this, and I, Child-of-Stars, shall be thy friend forever. But break the Vow, and I shall break thy City asunder, and drive thee forth into the wilderness to live like beasts, naked and comfortless, to sweat and toil beneath the lash of storms.*

And the people of the Lost Nation, and those who lived of Zarouk's band, bent their heads before the Glory and repeated again the Vow their ancestors had sworn, long ago.

*The Door I shall seal forever, that none may again be tempted to flee into Tomorrow, and the Keystone shall be riven into dust, aye, and that false replica made by the cunning of the priest. You shall dwell here in the past for all your days, you and your children and your children's children, far from strife and want and peril.*

And the twin seals were ground into dust before the eyes of all, and, far off at the head of the valley, a doorway veiled in glittering metallic mist closed, and was solid rock again, nevermore to open.

*My priesthood I withdraw from the line of Valarda, but not to chastise her for failing to restrain the warlike passions of her subjects. Instead, I bequeath it unto the child, Kiki, who hath partaken of my spirit and who hath close affinity with me. He in his time shall pass my spirit on to whomsoever he chooseth, that I may be served forever.*

Valarda bowed in submission, then raised her face to the Glory.

"And what of me and mine, Lord? What is your will?" she whispered.

The Glory looked down upon her, in all her beauty and humility, then looked to the strong, grim-faced Earthling who stood very near. And the Child-of-Stars laughed!

*You have love for each other, you two, after the ways of your flesh,* it said gently. *Why do you deny the passion written in your hearts? Go unto each other, my children, and make many fat babies! And you, Valarda, shall reign over this people as their Princess. And you, Earthling, shall rule beside her whom thy heart loveth. Be strong and fair and just and vigilant in that rule, for behold, among you there yet live those who were thine enemies, Zarouk and Thoh. See that you hold steady the thrones that Child-of-Stars hath given you.*

"We shall hold them, Lord," said Ryker. And it was a promise.

*Do so, then! . . . Love each other; rule in peace; and find happiness after the manner of your kind. Now I grow weary, I who have slept the ages by, dreaming of that which I shall never find, that which will ever remain unattainable . . . another like unto me to companion me through all the aeons to come. Leave me, now, my children, for I would return to my dreams, wherein alone I may find the happiness else denied me.*

And the Glory sank into the City, and the ground opened before it. But for a moment it lingered, lingered—

*But wake me, in just a little time—as you measure time—so that I may look upon the first of those fat babies. Now, farewell!*

The ground closed in thunder, and the Glory was gone.

And Ryker took Valarda's hand in his own, and they

214

went down from that height into their City, where Herzog and Melandron and Kiki and many others awaited them, to wed and to rule, to issue their commands and decrees. And, very likely, to live happily all their days, after the manner of their kind.

*And the evening and the morning were the seventh day.*

## SF'S FINEST WRITERS
## ARE PUBLISHED BY BERKLEY